PENGUIN BOOKS

The Prime of Miss Jean Brodie

Muriel Spark, D.B.E., C.Litt., (1918–2006) was born and educated in Edinburgh. A poet and novelist, she was best known for her stories and her many successful novels including *Memento Mori*, *The Prime of Miss Jean Brodie*, *The Driver's Seat*, *The Hothouse by the East River*, *Loitering with Intent*, *A Far Cry from Kensington*, *Symposium* and *The Finishing School*. She also wrote children's books; radio plays; a comedy (*Doctors of Philosophy*, first performed in London in 1962); biographies of nineteenth-century literary figures, including Mary Shelley and Emily Brontë; a volume of autobiography, *Curriculum Vitae*; and in 2004 published *All the Poems of Muriel Spark*.

For her long career of literary achievement, Dame Muriel Spark won international praise and many awards, including the David Cohen British Literature Award, the T. S. Eliot Award, the *Observer* Short Story Prize, the James Tait Black Memorial Prize, the Boccaccio Prize for European Literature, the Gold Pen Award, the first Enlightenment Award and the Italia Prize for dramatic radio. She was made an Honorary Member of the American Academy and Institute of Arts and Letters and a Commandeur de l'Ordre des Arts et des Lettres in France. She was given honorary doctorates of Letters from a number of universities, including London, Edinburgh and Oxford, and she was made the first Honorary Citizen of the historic Tuscan town of Civitella in Val di Chiana. Muriel Spark died in 2006.

The Prime of
Miss Jean Brodie

MURIEL SPARK

PENGUIN BOOKS

PENGUIN BOOKS

Published by the Penguin Group
Penguin Books Ltd, 80 Strand, London WC2R ORL, England
Penguin Group (USA) Inc., 375 Hudson Street, New York, New York 10014, USA
Penguin Group (Canada), 90 Eglinton Avenue East, Suite 700, Toronto, Ontario, Canada M4P 2Y3
(a division of Pearson Penguin Canada Inc.)
Penguin Ireland, 25 St Stephen's Green, Dublin 2, Ireland (a division of Penguin Books Ltd)
Penguin Group (Australia), 707 Collins Street, Melbourne, Victoria 3008, Australia
(a division of Pearson Australia Group Pty Ltd)
Penguin Books India Pvt Ltd, 11 Community Centre, Panchsheel Park, New Delhi – 110 017, India
Penguin Group (NZ), 67 Apollo Drive, Rosedale, Auckland 0632, New Zealand
(a division of Pearson New Zealand Ltd)
Penguin Books (South Africa) (Pty) Ltd, Block D, Rosebank Office Park,
181 Jan Smuts Avenue, Parktown North, Gauteng 2193, South Africa

Penguin Books Ltd, Registered Offices: 80 Strand, London WC2R ORL, England

www.penguin.com

First published in the United States of America by the *New Yorker* 1961
First published in Great Britain by Macmillan 1961
Published in Penguin Books 1965
Reissued in this edition 2013
001

Printed in Great Britain by Clays Ltd, St Ives plc

ISBN: 978-0-241-96400-2

www.greenpenguin.co.uk

MIX
Paper from
responsible sources
FSC™ C018179

Penguin Books is committed to a sustainable
future for our business, our readers and our planet.
This book is made from Forest Stewardship
Council™ certified paper.

ALWAYS LEARNING   **PEARSON**

Chapter One

The boys, as they talked to the girls from Marcia Blaine School, stood on the far side of their bicycles holding the handlebars, which established a protective fence of bicycle between the sexes, and the impression that at any moment the boys were likely to be away.

The girls could not take off their panama hats because this was not far from the school gates and hatlessness was an offence. Certain departures from the proper set of the hat on the head were overlooked in the case of fourth-form girls and upwards so long as nobody wore their hat at an angle. But there were other subtle variants from the ordinary rule of wearing the brim turned up at the back and down at the front. The five girls, standing very close to each other because of the boys, wore their hats each with a definite difference.

These girls formed the Brodie set. That was what they had been called even before the headmistress had given them the name, in scorn, when they had moved from the Junior to the Senior school at the age of twelve. At that time they had been immediately recognizable as Miss Brodie's pupils, being vastly informed on a lot of subjects irrelevant to the authorized curriculum, as the headmistress said, and useless to the school as a school. These girls were discovered to have heard of the Buchmanites and Mussolini, the Italian Renaissance painters, the advantages to the skin of cleansing cream and witch-hazel over honest soap and water, and the word 'menarche'; the interior decoration of the London house of the author of *Winnie the Pooh* had been described to them, as had the love lives of Charlotte Brontë and of Miss Brodie herself. They were aware of the existence of Einstein and the arguments of those who considered the Bible to be untrue. They knew the rudiments of astrology but not the date of the Battle of Flodden or the capital of Finland. All of the Brodie set, save one, counted on its fingers, as had Miss Brodie, with accurate results more or less.

By the time they were sixteen, and had reached the fourth form, and loitered beyond the gates after school, and had adapted themselves to the orthodox régime, they remained unmistakably Brodie, and were all famous in the school, which is to say they were held in suspicion and not much liking. They had no team spirit and very little in common with each other outside their continuing friendship with Jean Brodie. She still taught in the Junior department. She was held in great suspicion.

Marcia Blaine School for Girls was a day school which had been partially endowed in the middle of the nineteenth century by the wealthy widow of an Edinburgh bookbinder. She had been an admirer of Garibaldi before she died. Her manly portrait hung in the great hall, and was honoured every Founder's Day by a bunch of hard-wearing flowers such as chrysanthemums or dahlias. These were placed in a vase beneath the portrait, upon a lectern which also held an open Bible with the text underlined in red ink, 'O where shall I find a virtuous woman, for her price is above rubies.'

The girls who loitered beneath the tree, shoulder to shoulder, very close to each other because of the boys, were all famous for something. Now, at sixteen, Monica Douglas was a prefect, famous mostly for mathematics which she could do in her brain, and for her anger which, when it was lively enough, drove her to slap out to right and left. She had a very red nose, winter and summer, long dark plaits, and fat, peg-like legs. Since she had turned sixteen, Monica wore her panama hat rather higher on her head than normal, perched as if it were too small and as if she knew she looked grotesque in any case.

Rose Stanley was famous for sex. Her hat was placed quite unobtrusively on her blonde short hair, but she dented in the crown on either side.

Eunice Gardiner, small, neat, and famous for her spritely gymnastics and glamorous swimming, had the brim of her hat turned up at the front and down at the back.

Sandy Stranger wore it turned up all round and as far back on her head as it could possibly go; to assist this, she had attached to her hat a strip of elastic which went under the chin. Sometimes Sandy chewed this elastic and when it was chewed down she sewed on a new piece. She was merely notorious for her small, almost non-existent, eyes, but she was famous for her vowel sounds which, long ago in the long past, in the Junior school, had enraptured Miss Brodie. 'Well, come and recite for us please, because it has been a tiring day.'

> 'She left the web, she left the loom,
> She made three paces thro' the room,
> She saw the water-lily bloom,
> She saw the helmet and the plume,
> She look'd down to Camelot.'

'It lifts one up,' Miss Brodie usually said, passing her hand outwards from her breast towards the class of ten-year-old girls who were listening for the bell which would release them. 'Where there is no vision,' Miss Brodie had assured them, 'the people perish. Eunice, come and do a somersault in order that we may have comic relief.'

But now, the boys with their bicycles were cheerfully insulting Jenny Gray about her way of speech which she had got from her elocution classes. She was going to be an actress. She was Sandy's best friend. She wore her hat with the front brim bent sharply downwards; she was the prettiest and most graceful girl of the set, and this was her fame. 'Don't be a lout, Andrew,' she said with her uppish tone. There were three Andrews among the five boys, and these three Andrews now started mimicking Jenny: 'Don't be a lout, Andrew,' while the girls laughed beneath their bobbing panamas.

Along came Mary Macgregor, the last member of the set, whose fame rested on her being a silent lump, a nobody whom everybody could blame. With her was an outsider, Joyce Emily Hammond, the very rich girl, their delinquent, who had been recently sent to Blaine as a last hope, because no other school, no governess, could manage her. She still wore the green uniform of her old school. The others wore deep violet. The most she had done, so far, was to throw paper pellets sometimes at the singing master. She insisted on the use of her two names, Joyce Emily. This Joyce Emily was trying very hard to get into the famous set, and thought the two names might establish her as a something, but there was no chance of it and she could not see why.

Joyce Emily said, 'There's a teacher coming out,' and nodded towards the gates.

Two of the Andrews wheeled their bicycles out on to the road and departed. The other three boys remained defiantly, but looking the other way as if they might have stopped to admire the clouds on the Pentland Hills. The girls crowded round each other as if in discussion. 'Good afternoon,' said Miss Brodie when she approached the group. 'I haven't seen you for some days. I think we won't detain these young men and their bicycles. Good afternoon, boys.' The famous set moved off with her, and Joyce, the new delinquent, followed. 'I think I haven't met this new girl,' said Miss Brodie, looking closely at Joyce. And when they were introduced she said: 'Well, we must be on our way, my dear.'

Sandy looked back as Joyce Emily walked, and then skipped, leggy and uncontrolled for her age, in the opposite direction, and the Brodie set was left to their secret life as it had been six years ago in their childhood.

'I am putting old heads on your young shoulders,' Miss Brodie had told them at that time, 'and all my pupils are the crème de la crème.'

Sandy looked with her little screwed-up eyes at Monica's very red nose and remembered this saying as she followed the set in the wake of Miss Brodie.

'I should like you girls to come to supper tomorrow night,' Miss Brodie said. 'Make sure you are free.'

'The Dramatic Society . . .' murmured Jenny.

'Send an excuse,' said Miss Brodie. 'I have to consult you about a new plot which is afoot to force me to resign. Needless to say, I shall not resign.' She spoke calmly as she always did in spite of her forceful words.

Miss Brodie never discussed her affairs with the other members of the staff, but only with those former pupils whom she had trained up in her confidence. There had been previous plots to remove her from Blaine, which had been foiled.

'It has been suggested again that I should apply for a post at one of the progressive schools, where my methods would be more suited to the system than they are at Blaine. But I shall not apply for a post at a crank school. I shall remain at this education factory. There needs must be a leaven in the lump. Give me a girl at an impressionable age, and she is mine for life.'

The Brodie set smiled in understanding of various kinds.

Miss Brodie forced her brown eyes to flash as a meaningful accompaniment to her quiet voice. She looked a mighty woman with her dark Roman profile in the sun. The Brodie set did not for a moment doubt that she would prevail. As soon expect Julius Caesar to apply for a job at a crank school as Miss Brodie. She would never resign. If the authorities wanted to get rid of her she would have to be assassinated.

'Who are the gang, this time?' said Rose, who was famous for sex-appeal.

'We shall discuss tomorrow night the persons who oppose me,' said Miss Brodie. 'But rest assured they shall not succeed.'

'No,' said everyone. 'No, of course they won't.'

'Not while I am in my prime,' she said. 'These years are still the years of my prime. It is important to recognize the years of one's prime, always remember that. Here is my tram-car. I dare say I'll not get a seat. This is nineteen-thirty-six. The age of chivalry is past.'

Six years previously, Miss Brodie had led her new class into the garden for a history lesson underneath the big elm. On the way through the school corridors they passed the headmistress's study. The door was wide open, the room was empty.

'Little girls,' said Miss Brodie, 'come and observe this.'

They clustered round the open door while she pointed to a large poster pinned with drawing-pins on the opposite wall within the room. It depicted a man's big face. Under-neath were the words 'Safety First'.

'This is Stanley Baldwin who got in as Prime Minister and got out again ere long,' said Miss Brodie. 'Miss Mackay retains him on the wall because she believes in the slogan "Safety First". But Safety does not come first. Good-ness, Truth and Beauty come first. Follow me.'

This was the first intimation, to the girls, of an odds between Miss Brodie and the rest of the teaching staff. Indeed, to some of them, it was the first time they had realized it was possible for people glued together in grown-up authority to differ at all. Taking inward note of this, and with the exhilarating feeling of being in on the faint smell of row, without being endangered by it, they followed dangerous Miss Brodie into the secure shade of the elm.

Often, that sunny autumn, when the weather permitted, the small girls took their lessons seated on three benches arranged about the elm.

'Hold up your books,' said Miss Brodie quite often that autumn, 'prop them up in your hands, in case of intruders.

If there are any intruders, we are doing our history lesson . . . our poetry . . . English grammar.'

The small girls held up their books with their eyes not on them, but on Miss Brodie.

'Meantime I will tell you about my last summer holiday in Egypt . . . I will tell you about care of the skin, and of the hands . . . about the Frenchman I met in the train to Biarritz . . . and I must tell you about the Italian paintings I saw. Who is the greatest Italian painter?'

'Leonardo da Vinci, Miss Brodie.'

'That is incorrect. The answer is Giotto, he is my favourite.'

Some days it seemed to Sandy that Miss Brodie's chest was flat, no bulges at all, but straight as her back. On other days her chest was breast-shaped and large, very noticeable, something for Sandy to sit and peer at through her tiny eyes while Miss Brodie on a day of lessons indoors stood erect, with her brown head held high, staring out of the window like Joan of Arc as she spoke.

'I have frequently told you, and the holidays just past have convinced me, that my prime has truly begun. One's prime is elusive. You little girls, when you grow up, must be on the alert to recognize your prime at whatever time of your life it may occur. You must then live it to the full. Mary, what have you got under your desk, what are you looking at?'

Mary sat lump-like and too stupid to invent something. She was too stupid ever to tell a lie; she didn't know how to cover up.

'A comic, Miss Brodie,' she said.

'Do you mean a comedian, a droll?'

Everyone tittered.

'A comic paper,' said Mary.

'A comic paper, forsooth. How old are you?'

'Ten, ma'am.'

'You are too old for comic papers at ten. Give it to me.'

Miss Brodie looked at the coloured sheets. '*Tiger Tim's* forsooth,' she said, and threw it into the waste-paper basket. Perceiving all eyes upon it she lifted it out of the basket, tore it up beyond redemption and put it back again.

'Attend to me, girls. One's prime is the moment one was born for. Now that my prime has begun – Sandy, your attention is wandering. What have I been talking about?'

'Your prime, Miss Brodie.'

'If anyone comes along,' said Miss Brodie, 'in the course of the following lesson, remember that it is the hour for English grammar. Meantime I will tell you a little of my life when I was younger than I am now, though six years older than the man himself.'

She leaned against the elm. It was one of the last autumn days when the leaves were falling in little gusts. They fell on the children who were thankful for this excuse to wriggle and for the allowable movements in brushing the leaves from their hair and laps.

'Season of mists and mellow fruitfulness. I was engaged to a young man at the beginning of the War but he fell on Flanders' Field,' said Miss Brodie. 'Are you thinking, Sandy, of doing a day's washing?'

'No, Miss Brodie.'

'Because you have got your sleeves rolled up. I won't have to do with girls who roll up the sleeves of their blouses, however fine the weather. Roll them down at once, we are civilized beings. He fell the week before Armistice was declared. He fell like an autumn leaf, although he was only twenty-two years of age. When we go indoors we shall look on the map at Flanders, and the spot where my lover was laid before you were born. He was poor. He came from Ayrshire, a countryman, but a hard-working and clever scholar. He said, when he asked me to marry him, "We shall have to drink water and walk slow." That was Hugh's country way of expressing that we would live quietly. We shall drink water and walk slow. What does the saying signify, Rose?'

'That you would live quietly, Miss Brodie,' said Rose Stanley who six years later had a great reputation for sex.

The story of Miss Brodie's felled fiancé was well on its way when the headmistress, Miss Mackay, was seen to approach across the lawn. Tears had already started to drop from Sandy's little pig-like eyes and Sandy's tears now affected her friend Jenny, later famous in the school for her beauty, who gave a sob and groped up the leg of her knickers for her handkerchief. 'Hugh was killed,' said Miss Brodie, 'a week before the Armistice. After that there was a general election and people were saying "Hang the Kaiser!" Hugh was one of the Flowers of the Forest, lying in his grave.' Rose Stanley had now begun to weep. Sandy slid her wet eyes sideways, watching the advance of Miss Mackay, head and shoulders forward, across the lawn.

'I am come to see you and I have to be off,' she said. 'What are you little girls crying for?'

'They are moved by a story I have been telling them. We are having a history lesson,' said Miss Brodie, catching a falling leaf neatly in her hand as she spoke.

'Crying over a story at ten years of age!' said Miss Mackay to the girls who had stragglingly risen from the benches, still dazed with Hugh the warrior. 'I am only come to see you and I must be off. Well, girls, the new term has begun. I hope you all had a splendid summer holiday and I look forward to seeing your splendid essays on how you spent them. You shouldn't be crying over history at the age of ten. My word!'

'You did well,' said Miss Brodie to the class, when Miss Mackay had gone, 'not to answer the question put to you. It is well, when in difficulties, to say never a word, neither black nor white. Speech is silver but silence is golden. Mary, are you listening? What was I saying?'

Mary Macgregor, lumpy, with merely two eyes, a nose

and a mouth like a snowman, who was later famous for being stupid and always to blame and who, at the age of twenty-three, lost her life in a hotel fire, ventured, 'Golden.'

'What did I say was golden?'

Mary cast her eyes around her and up above. Sandy whispered, 'The falling leaves.'

'The falling leaves,' said Mary.

'Plainly,' said Miss Brodie, 'you were not listening to me. If only you small girls would listen to me I would make of you the crème de la crème.'

Chapter Two

Mary Macgregor, although she lived into her twenty-fourth year, never quite realized that Jean Brodie's confidences were not shared with the rest of the staff and that her love-story was given out only to her pupils. She had not thought much about Jean Brodie, certainly never disliked her, when, a year after the outbreak of the Second World War, she joined the Wrens, and was clumsy and incompetent, and was much blamed. On one occasion of real misery – when her first and last boy-friend, a corporal whom she had known for two weeks, deserted her by failing to turn up at an appointed place and failing to come near her again – she thought back to see if she had ever really been happy in her life; it occurred to her then that the first years with Miss Brodie, sitting listening to all those stories and opinions which had nothing to do with the ordinary world, had been the happiest time of her life. She thought this briefly, and never again referred her mind to Miss Brodie, but had got over her misery, and had relapsed into her habitual slow bewilderment, before she died while on leave in Cumberland in a fire in the hotel. Back and forth along the corridors ran Mary Macgregor, through the thickening smoke. She ran one way; then, turning, the other way; and at either end the blast furnace of the fire met her. She heard no screams, for the roar of the fire drowned the screams; she gave no scream, for the smoke was choking her. She ran into somebody on her third turn, stumbled and died. But at the beginning of the nineteen-thirties, when Mary Macgregor was ten, there she was sitting blankly among Miss Brodie's pupils. 'Who has spilled ink on the floor – was it you, Mary?'

'I don't know, Miss Brodie.'

'I dare say it was you. I've never come across such a clumsy girl. And if you can't take an interest in what I am saying, please try to look as if you do.'

These were the days that Mary Macgregor, on looking back, found to be the happiest days of her life.

Sandy Stranger had a feeling at the time that they were supposed to be the happiest days of her life, and on her tenth birthday she said so to her best friend Jenny Gray who had been asked to tea at Sandy's house. The speciality of the feast was pineapple cubes with cream, and the speciality of the day was that they were left to themselves. To Sandy the unfamilar pineapple had the authentic taste and appearance of happiness and she focused her small eyes closely on the pale gold cubes before she scooped them up in her spoon, and she thought the sharp taste on her tongue was that of a special happiness, which was nothing to do with eating, and was different from the happiness of play that one enjoyed unawares. Both girls saved the cream to the last, then ate it in spoonfuls.

'Little girls, you are going to be the crème de la crème,' said Sandy, and Jenny spluttered her cream into her handkerchief.

'You know,' Sandy said, 'these are supposed to be the happiest days of our lives.'

'Yes, they are always saying that,' Jenny said. 'They say, make the most of your schooldays because you never know what lies ahead of you.'

'Miss Brodie says prime is best,' Sandy said.

'Yes, but she never got married like our mothers and fathers.'

'They don't have primes,' said Sandy.

'They have sexual intercourse,' Jenny said.

The little girls paused, because this was still a stupendous thought, and one which they had only lately lit upon; the very phrase and its meaning were new. It was quite unbelievable. Sandy said, then, 'Mr Lloyd had a baby last week. He must have committed sex with his wife.' This idea was easier to cope with and they laughed screamingly into their pink paper napkins. Mr Lloyd was the Art master to the Senior girls.

'Can you *see* it happening?' Jenny whispered.

Sandy screwed her eyes even smaller in the effort of seeing with her mind. 'He would be wearing his pyjamas,' she whispered back.

The girls rocked with mirth, thinking of one-armed Mr Lloyd, in his solemnity, striding into school.

Then Jenny said, 'You do it on the spur of the moment. That's how it happens.'

Jenny was a reliable source of information, because a girl employed by her father in his grocer shop had recently been found to be pregnant, and Jenny had picked up some fragments of the ensuing fuss. Having confided her finds to Sandy, they had embarked on a course of research which they called 'research', piecing together clues from remembered conversations illicitly overheard, and passages from the big dictionaries.

'It all happens in a flash,' Jenny said. 'It happened to Teenie when she was out walking at Puddocky with her boy friend. Then they had to get married.'

'You would think the urge would have passed by the time she got her *clothes* off,' Sandy said. By 'clothes' she definitely meant to imply knickers, but 'knickers' was rude in this scientific context.

'Yes, that's what I can't understand,' said Jenny.

Sandy's mother looked round the door and said, 'Enjoying yourselves, darlings?' Over her shoulder appeared the head of Jenny's mother. 'My word,' said Jenny's mother, looking at the tea-table, 'they've been tucking in!'

Sandy felt offended and belittled by this; it was as if the main idea of the party had been the food.

'What would you like to do now?' Sandy's mother said.

Sandy gave her mother a look of secret ferocity which meant: you promised to leave us all on our own, and a promise is a promise, you know it's very bad to break a promise to a child, you might ruin all my life by breaking your promise, it's my birthday.

Sandy's mother backed away bearing Jenny's mother with her. 'Let's leave them to themselves,' she said. 'Just enjoy yourselves, darlings.'

Sandy was sometimes embarrassed by her mother being English and calling her 'darling', not like the mothers of Edinburgh who said 'dear'. Sandy's mother had a flashy winter coat trimmed with fluffy fox fur like the Duchess of York's, while the other mothers wore tweed or, at the most, musquash that would do them all their days.

It had been raining and the ground was too wet for them to go and finish digging the hole to Australia, so the girls lifted the tea-table with all its festal relics over to the corner of the room. Sandy opened the lid of the piano stool and extracted a notebook from between two sheaves of music. On the first page of the notebook was written,

The Mountain Eyrie
by
Sandy Stranger and Jenny Gray

This was a story, still in the process of composition, about Miss Brodie's lover, Hugh Carruthers. He had not been killed in the war, that was a mistake in the telegram. He had come back from the war and called to inquire for Miss Brodie at school, where the first person whom he encountered was Miss Mackay, the headmistress. She had informed him that Miss Brodie did not desire to see him, she loved another. With a bitter, harsh laugh, Hugh went and made his abode in a mountain eyrie, where, wrapped in a leather jacket, he had been discovered one day by Sandy and Jenny. At the present stage in the story Hugh was holding Sandy captive but Jenny had escaped by night and was attempting to find her way down the mountainside in the dark. Hugh was preparing to pursue her.

Sandy took a pencil from a drawer in the sideboard and continued:

'Hugh!' Sandy beseeched him, 'I swear to you before all I hold sacred that Miss Brodie has never loved another, and she awaits you below, praying and hoping in her prime. If you will let Jenny go, she will bring back your lover Jean Brodie to you and you will see her with your own eyes and hold her in your arms after these twelve long years and a day.'

His black eye flashed in the lamplight of the hut. 'Back, girl!' he cried, 'and do not bar my way. Well do I know that yon girl Jenny will report my whereabouts to my mocking erstwhile fiancée. Well do I know that you are both spies sent by her that she might mock. Stand back from the door, I say!'

'Never!' said Sandy, placing her young lithe body squarely in front of the latch and her arm through the bolt. Her large eyes flashed with an azure light of appeal.

Sandy handed the pencil to Jenny. 'It's your turn,' she said.

Jenny wrote: With one movement he flung her to the farthest end of the hut and strode out into the moonlight and his strides made light of the drifting snow.

'Put in about his boots,' said Sandy.

Jenny wrote: His high boots flashed in the moonlight.

'There are too many moonlights,' Sandy said, 'but we can sort that later when it comes to publication.'

'Oh, but it's a secret, Sandy!' said Jenny.

'I know that,' Sandy said. 'Don't worry, we won't publish it till our prime.'

'Do you think Miss Brodie ever had sexual intercourse with Hugh?' said Jenny.

'She would have had a baby, wouldn't she?'

'I don't know.'

'I don't think they did anything like that,' said Sandy. 'Their love was above all that.'

'Miss Brodie said they clung to each other with passionate abandon on his last leave.'

'I don't think they took their clothes off, though,' Sandy said, 'do you?'

'No. I can't see it,' said Jenny.

'I wouldn't like to have sexual intercourse,' Sandy said.

'Neither would I. I'm going to marry a pure person.'

'Have a toffee.'

They ate their sweets, sitting on the carpet. Sandy put some coal on the fire and the light spurted up, reflecting on Jenny's ringlets. 'Let's be witches by the fire, like we were at Hallowe'en.'

They sat in the twilight eating toffees and incanting witches' spells. Jenny said, 'There's a Greek god at the museum standing up with nothing on. I saw it last Sunday afternoon but I was with Auntie Kate and I didn't have a chance to *look* properly.'

'Let's go to the museum next Sunday,' Sandy said. 'It's research.'

'Would you be allowed to go alone with me?'

Sandy, who was notorious for not being allowed to go out and about without a grown-up person, said, 'I don't think so. Perhaps we could get someone to take us.'

'We could ask Miss Brodie.'

Miss Brodie frequently took the little girls to the art galleries and museums, so this seemed feasible.

'But suppose,' said Sandy, 'she won't let us look at the statue if it's naked.'

'I don't think she would notice that it was naked,' Jenny said. 'She just wouldn't see its thingummyjig.'

'I know,' said Sandy. 'Miss Brodie's above all that.'

It was time for Jenny to go home with her mother, all the way in the tram car through the haunted November twilight of Edinburgh across the Dean Bridge. Sandy waved from the window, and wondered if Jenny, too, had the feeling of leading a double life, fraught with problems that even a millionaire did not have to face. It was well known that millionaires led double lives. The evening paper rattle-snaked its way through the letter box and there was suddenly a six-o'clock feeling in the house.

Miss Brodie was reciting poetry to the class at a quarter to four, to raise their minds before they went home. Miss Brodie's eyes were half shut and her head was thrown back:

> 'In the stormy east wind straining,
> The pale yellow woods were waning,
> The broad stream in his banks complaining,
> Heavily the low sky raining
>   Over tower'd Camelot.'

Sandy watched Miss Brodie through her little pale eyes, screwed them smaller and shut her lips tight.

Rose Stanley was pulling threads from the girdle of her gym tunic. Jenny was enthralled by the poem, her lips were parted, she was never bored. Sandy was never bored, but she had to lead a double life of her own in order never to be bored.

> Down she came and found a boat
> Beneath a willow left afloat,
> And round about the prow she wrote
> *The Lady of Shalott.*

'By what means did your Ladyship write these words?' Sandy inquired in her mind with her lips shut tight.

'There was a pot of white paint and a brush which happened to be standing upon the grassy verge,' replied the Lady of Shalott graciously. 'It was left there no doubt by some heedless member of the Unemployed.'

'Alas, and in all that rain!' said Sandy for want of something better to say, while Miss Brodie's voice soared up to the ceiling, and curled round the feet of the Senior girls upstairs.

The Lady of Shalott placed a white hand on Sandy's shoulder and gazed at her for a space. 'That one so young and beautiful should be so ill-fated in love!' she said in low sad tones.

'What can be the meaning of these words?' cried Sandy in alarm, with her little eyes screwed on Miss Brodie and her lips shut tight.

Miss Brodie said: 'Sandy, are you in pain?'

Sandy looked astonished.

'You girls,' said Miss Brodie, 'must learn to cultivate an expression of composure. It is one of the best assets of a woman, an expression of composure, come foul, come fair. Regard the Mona Lisa over yonder!'

All heads turned to look at the reproduction which Miss Brodie had brought back from her travels and pinned on the wall. Mona Lisa in her prime smiled in steady composure even though she had just come from the dentist and her lower jaw was swollen.

'She is older than the rocks on which she sits. Would that I had been given charge of you girls when you were seven. I sometimes fear it's too late, now. If you had been mine when you were seven you would have been the crème de la crème. Sandy, come and read some stanzas and let us hear your vowel sounds.'

Sandy, being half-English, made the most of her vowels, it was her only fame. Rose Stanley was not yet famous for sex, and it was not she but Eunice Gardiner who had approached Sandy and Jenny with a Bible, pointing out the words, 'The babe leapt in her womb'. Sandy and Jenny said she was dirty and threatened to tell on her. Jenny was already famous for her prettiness, and she had a sweet voice, so that Mr Lowther, who came to teach singing, would watch her admiringly as she sang 'Come see where golden-hearted spring . . .'; and he twitched her ringlets, the more daringly since Miss Brodie always stayed with her pupils during the singing lesson. He twitched her ringlets and looked at Miss Brodie like a child showing off its tricks and almost as if testing Miss Brodie to see if she were at all willing to conspire in his un-Edinburgh conduct.

Mr Lowther was small, with a long body and short legs. His hair and moustache were red-gold. He curled his hand round the back of his ear and inclined his head towards each girl to test her voice. 'Sing ah!'

'Ah!' sang Jenny, high and pure as the sea maiden of the Hebrides whom Sandy had been talking about. But her eyes swivelled over to catch Sandy's.

Miss Brodie ushered the girls from the music room and, gathering them about her, said, 'You girls are my vocation. If I were to receive a proposal of marriage tomorrow from the Lord Lyon King-of-Arms I would decline it. I am dedicated to you in my prime. Form a single file, now, please, and walk with your heads up, *up*, like Sybil Thorndike, a woman of noble mien.'

Sandy craned back her head, pointed her freckled nose in the air and fixed her little pig-like eyes on the ceiling as she walked along in the file.

'What are you doing, Sandy?'

'Walking like Sybil Thorndike, ma'am.'

'One day, Sandy, you will go too far.'

Sandy looked hurt and puzzled.

'Yes,' said Miss Brodie, 'I have my eye upon you, Sandy. I observe a frivolous nature. I fear you will never belong to life's élite or, as one might say, the crème de la crème.'

When they had returned to the classroom Rose Stanley said, 'I've got ink on my blouse.'

'Go to the science room and have the stain removed; but remember it is very bad for the tussore.'

Sometimes the girls would put a little spot of ink on a sleeve of their tussore silk blouses so that they might be sent to the science room in the Senior school. There a thrilling teacher, a Miss Lockhart, wearing a white overall, with her grey short hair set back in waves from a tanned and weathered golfer's face, would pour a small drop of white liquid from a large jar on to a piece of cotton wool. With this she would dab the ink-spot on the sleeve, silently holding the girl's arm, intently absorbed in the task. Rose Stanley went to the science room with her inky blouse only because she was bored, but Sandy and Jenny got ink on their blouses at discreet intervals of four weeks, so that they could go and have their arms held by Miss Lockhart who seemed to carry six inches of pure air around her person wherever she moved in that strange-smelling room. This long room was her natural setting and she had lost something of her quality when Sandy saw her walking from the school in her box-pleat tweeds over to her sports car like an ordinary teacher. Miss Lockhart in the science room was to Sandy something apart, surrounded by three lanes of long benches set out with jars half-full of coloured crystals and powders and liquids, ochre and bronze and metal grey and cobalt blue, glass vessels of curious shapes, bulbous, or with pipe-like stems. Only once when Sandy went to the science room was there a lesson in progress. The older girls, big girls, some with bulging chests, were standing in couples at the benches, with gas jets burning before them. They held a glass tube full of green stuff in their hands and were dancing the tube in the flame, dozens of dancing green tubes and flames, all along the benches. The bare winter top branches of the trees brushed the windows of this long room, and beyond that was the cold winter sky with a huge red sun. Sandy, on that occasion, had the presence of mind to remember that her schooldays were supposed to be the happiest days of her life and she took the compelling news back to Jenny that the Senior school was going to be marvellous and Miss Lockhart was beautiful.

'All the girls in the science room were doing just as they

liked,' said Sandy, 'and that's what they were supposed to be doing.'

'We do a lot of what we like in Miss Brodie's class,' Jenny said. 'My mummy says Miss Brodie gives us too much freedom.'

'She's not supposed to give us freedom, she's supposed to give us lessons,' said Sandy. 'But the science class is supposed to be free, it's allowed.'

'Well, I like being in Miss Brodie's,' Jenny said.

'So do I,' Sandy said. 'She takes an interest in our general knowledge, my mother says.'

All the same, the visits to the science room were Sandy's most secret joy, and she calculated very carefully the intervals between one ink-spot and another, so that there should be no suspicion on Miss Brodie's part that the spots were not an accident. Miss Lockhart would hold her arm and carefully dab the ink-stain on her sleeve while Sandy stood enthralled by the long room which was this science teacher's rightful place, and by the lawful glamour of everything there. It was on the occasion when Rose Stanley, after the singing lesson, was sent to the science room to get ink off her blouse that Miss Brodie told her class,

'You must be more careful with your ink. I can't have my girls going up and down to the science room like this. We must keep our good name.'

She added, 'Art is greater than science. Art comes first, and then science.'

The large map had been rolled down over the blackboard because they had started the geography lesson. Miss Brodie turned with her pointer to show where Alaska lay. But she turned again to the class and said: 'Art and religion first; then philosophy; lastly science. That is the order of the great subjects of life, that's their order of importance.'

This was the first winter of the two years that this class spent with Miss Brodie. It had turned nineteen-thirty-one.

Miss Brodie had already selected her favourites, or rather those whom she could trust; or rather those whose parents she could trust not to lodge complaints about the more advanced and seditious aspects of her educational policy, these parents being either too enlightened to complain or too unenlightened, or too awed by their good fortune in getting their girls' education at endowed rates, or too trusting to question the value of what their daughters were learning at this school of sound reputation. Miss Brodie's special girls were taken home to tea and bidden not to tell the others, they were taken into her confidence, they understood her private life and her feud with the headmistress and the allies of the headmistress. They learned what troubles in her career Miss Brodie had encountered on their behalf. 'It is for the sake of you girls – my influence, now, in the years of my prime.' This was the beginning of the Brodie set. Eunice Gardiner was so quiet at first, it was difficult to see why she had been drawn in by Miss Brodie. But eventually she cut capers for the relief and amusement of the tea-parties, doing cartwheels on the carpet. 'You are an Ariel,' said Miss Brodie. Then Eunice began to chatter. She was not allowed to do cartwheels on Sundays, for in many ways Miss Brodie was an Edinburgh spinster of the deepest dye. Eunice Gardiner did somersaults on the mat only at Saturday gatherings before high teas, or afterwards on Miss Brodie's kitchen linoleum, while the other girls were washing up and licking honey from the depleted comb off their fingers as they passed it over to be put away in the food cupboard. It was twenty-eight years after Eunice did the splits in Miss Brodie's flat that she, who had become a nurse and married a doctor, said to her husband one evening:

'Next year when we go for the Festival –'

'Yes?'

She was making a wool rug, pulling at a different stitch.

'Yes?' he said.

'When we go to Edinburgh,' she said, 'remind me while we're there to go and visit Miss Brodie's grave.'

'Who was Miss Brodie?'

'A teacher of mine, she was full of culture. She was an Edinburgh Festival all on her own. She used to give us teas at her flat and tell us about her prime.'

'Prime what?'

'Her prime of life. She fell for an Egyptian courier once, on her travels, and came back and told us all about it. She had a few favourites. I was one of them. I did the splits and made her laugh, you know.'

'I always knew your upbringing was a bit peculiar.'

'But she wasn't mad. She was as sane as anything. She knew exactly what she was doing. She told us all about her love life, too.'

'Let's have it then.'

'Oh, it's a long story. She was just a spinster. I must take flowers to her grave – I wonder if I could find it?'

'When did she die?'

'Just after the war. She was retired by then. Her retirement was rather a tragedy, she was forced to retire before time. The head never liked her. There's a long story attached to Miss Brodie's retirement. She was betrayed by one of her own girls, we were called the Brodie set. I never found out which one betrayed her.'

It is time now to speak of the long walk through the old parts of Edinburgh where Miss Brodie took her set, dressed in their deep violet coats and black velour hats with the green and white crest, one Friday in March when the school's central heating system had broken down and everyone else had been muffled up and sent home. The wind blew from the icy Forth and the sky was loaded with forthcoming snow. Mary Macgregor walked with Sandy because Jenny had gone home. Monica Douglas, later famous for being able to do real mathematics in her head, and for her anger, walked behind them with her dark red face, broad nose and dark pigtails falling from her black hat and her legs already shaped like pegs in their black wool stockings. By her side walked Rose Stanley, tall and blonde with a yellow-pale skin, who had not yet won her reputation for sex, and whose conversation was all about trains, cranes, motor cars, Meccanos, and other boys' affairs. She was not interested in the works of engines or the constructive powers of the Meccanos, but she knew their names, the variety of colours in which they came, the makes of motor cars and their horse-power, the various prices of the Meccano sets. She was also an energetic climber of walls and trees. And although these concerns at Rose Stanley's eleventh year marked her as a tomboy, they did not go deep into her femininity and it was her superficial knowledge of these topics alone, as if they had been a conscious preparation, which stood her in good stead a few years later with the boys.

With Rose walked Miss Brodie, head up, like Sybil Thorndike, her nose arched and proud. She wore her loose brown tweed coat with the beaver collar tightly buttoned, her brown felt hat with the brim up at one side and down at the other. Behind Miss Brodie, last in the group, little Eunice Gardiner who, twenty-eight years later, said of Miss Brodie, 'I must visit her grave', gave a skip between each of her walking steps as if she might even break into pirouettes on the pavement, so that Miss Brodie, turning round, said from time to time, 'Now, Eunice!' And, from time to time again, Miss Brodie would fall behind to keep Eunice company.

Sandy, who had been reading *Kidnapped*, was having a conversation with the hero, Alan Breck, and was glad to be with Mary Macgregor because it was not necessary to talk to Mary.

'Mary, you may speak quietly to Sandy.'

'Sandy won't talk to me,' said Mary who later, in that hotel fire, ran hither and thither till she died.

'Sandy cannot talk to you if you are so stupid and

disagreeable. Try to wear an agreeable expression at least, Mary.'

'Sandy, you must take this message o'er the heather to the Macphersons,' said Alan Breck. 'My life depends upon it, and the Cause no less.'

'I shall never fail you, Alan Breck,' said Sandy. 'Never.'

'Mary,' said Miss Brodie, from behind, 'please try not to lag behind Sandy.'

Sandy kept pacing ahead, fired on by Alan Breck whose ardour and thankfulness, as Sandy prepared to set off across the heather, had reached touching proportions.

Mary tried to keep up with her. They were crossing the Meadows, a gusty expanse of common land, glaring green under the snowy sky. Their destination was the Old Town, for Miss Brodie had said they should see where history had been lived; and their route had brought them to the Middle Meadow Walk.

Eunice, unaccompanied at the back, began to hop to a rhyme which she repeated to herself:

> Edinburgh, Leith,
> Portobello, Musselburgh
> *And* Dalkeith.

Then she changed to the other foot.

> Edinburgh, Leith ...

Miss Brodie turned round and hushed her, then called forward to Mary Macgregor who was staring at an Indian student who was approaching,

'Mary, don't you *want* to walk tidily?'

'Mary,' said Sandy, 'stop staring at the brown man.'

The nagged child looked numbly at Sandy and tried to quicken her pace. But Sandy was walking unevenly, in little spurts forward and little halts, as Alan Breck began to sing to her his ditty before she took to the heather to deliver the message that was going to save Alan's life. He sang:

This is the song of the sword of Alan:
The smith made it,
The fire set it;
Now it shines in the hands of Alan Breck.

Then Alan Breck clapped her shoulder and said, 'Sandy, you are a brave lass and want nothing in courage that any King's man might possess.'

'Don't walk so fast,' mumbled Mary.

'You aren't walking with your head up,' said Sandy. 'Keep it up, up.'

Then suddenly Sandy wanted to be kind to Mary Macgregor, and thought of the possibilities of feeling nice from being nice to Mary instead of blaming her. Miss Brodie's voice from behind was saying to Rose Stanley, 'You are all heroines in the making. Britain must be a fit country for heroines to live in. The League of Nations ...' The sound of Miss Brodie's presence, just when it was on the tip of Sandy's tongue to be nice to Mary Macgregor, arrested the urge. Sandy looked back at her companions, and understood them as a body with Miss Brodie for the head. She perceived herself, the absent Jenny, the ever-blamed Mary, Rose, Eunice, and Monica, all in a frightening little moment, in unified compliance to the destiny of Miss Brodie, as if God had willed them to birth for that purpose.

She was even more frightened then, by her temptation to be nice to Mary Macgregor, since by this action she would separate herself, and be lonely, and blameable in a more dreadful way than Mary who, although officially the faulty one, was at least inside Miss Brodie's category of heroines in the making. So, for good fellowship's sake, Sandy said to Mary, 'I wouldn't be walking with *you* if Jenny was here.' And Mary said, 'I know.' Then Sandy started to hate herself again and to nag on and on at Mary, with the feeling that if you did a thing a lot of times, you made it into a right thing. Mary started to cry, but quietly, so that Miss Brodie could not see. Sandy was unable to cope and decided to stride on and be a married lady having an argument with her husband:

'Well, Colin, it's rather hard on a woman when the lights have fused and there isn't a man in the house.'

'Dearest Sandy, *how* was I to know . . .'

As they came to the end of the Meadows a group of Girl Guides came by. Miss Brodie's brood, all but Mary, walked past with eyes ahead. Mary stared at the dark blue big girls with their regimented vigorous look and broader accents of speech than the Brodie girls used when in Miss Brodie's presence. They passed, and Sandy said to Mary, 'It's rude to stare.' And Mary said, 'I wasn't staring.' Meanwhile Miss Brodie was being questioned by the girls behind on the question of the Brownies and the Girl Guides, for quite a lot of the other girls in the Junior School were Brownies.

'For those who like that sort of thing,' said Miss Brodie in her best Edinburgh voice, 'that is the sort of thing they like.'

So Brownies and Guides were ruled out. Sandy recalled Miss Brodie's admiration for Mussolini's marching troops, and the picture she had brought back from Italy showing the triumphant march of the black uniforms in Rome.

'These are the fascisti,' said Miss Brodie, and spelt it out. 'What are these men, Rose?'

'The fascisti, Miss Brodie.'

They were dark as anything and all marching in the straightest of files, with their hands raised at the same angle, while Mussolini stood on a platform like a gym teacher or a Guides mistress and watched them. Mussolini had put an end to unemployment with his fascisti and there was no litter in the streets. It occurred to Sandy, there at the end of the Middle Meadow Walk, that the Brodie set was Miss Brodie's fascisti, not to the naked eye, marching along, but all knit together for her need and in another way, marching along. That was all right, but it seemed, too, that Miss

Brodie's disapproval of the Girl Guides had jealousy in it, there was an inconsistency, a fault. Perhaps the Guides were too much of a rival fascisti, and Miss Brodie could not bear it. Sandy thought she might see about joining the Brownies. Then the group-fright seized her again, and it was necessary to put the idea aside, because she loved Miss Brodie.

'We make good company for each other, Sandy,' said Alan Breck, crunching beneath his feet the broken glass among the blood on the floor of the ship's roundhouse. And taking a knife from the table, he cut off one of the silver buttons from his coat. 'Wherever you show that button,' he said, 'the friends of Alan Breck will come around you.'

'We turn to the right,' said Miss Brodie.

They approached the Old Town which none of the girls had properly seen before, because none of their parents was so historically minded as to be moved to conduct their young into the reeking network of slums which the Old Town constituted in those years. The Canongate, The Grassmarket, The Lawnmarket, were names which betokened a misty region of crime and desperation: 'Lawnmarket Man Jailed.' Only Eunice Gardiner and Monica Douglas had already traversed the High Street on foot on the Royal Mile from the Castle or Holyrood. Sandy had been taken to Holyrood in an uncle's car and had seen the bed, too short and too broad, where Mary Queen of Scots had slept, and the tiny room, smaller than their own scullery at home, where the Queen had played cards with Rizzio.

Now they were in a great square, the Grassmarket, with the Castle, which was in any case everywhere, rearing between a big gap in the houses where the aristocracy used to live. It was Sandy's first experience of a foreign country, which intimates itself by its new smells and shapes and its new poor. A man sat on the icy-cold pavement; he just sat.

A crowd of children, some without shoes, were playing some fight game, and some boys shouted after Miss Brodie's violet-clad company, with words that the girls had not heard before, but rightly understood to be obscene. Children and women with shawls came in and out of the dark closes. Sandy found she was holding Mary's hand in her bewilderment, all the girls were holding hands, while Miss Brodie talked of history. Into the High Street, and 'John Knox,' said Miss Brodie, 'was an embittered man. He could never be at ease with the gay French Queen. We of Edinburgh owe a lot to the French. We are Europeans.' The smell was amazingly terrible. In the middle of the road farther up the High Street a crowd was gathered. 'Walk past quietly,' said Miss Brodie.

A man and a woman stood in the midst of the crowd which had formed a ring round them. They were shouting at each other and the man hit the woman twice across the head. Another woman, very little, with cropped black hair, a red face and a big mouth, came forward and took the man by the arm. She said:

'I'll be your man.'

From time to time throughout her life Sandy pondered this, for she was certain that the little woman's words were 'I'll be your man', not 'I'll be your woman', and it was never explained.

And many times throughout her life Sandy knew with a shock, when speaking to people whose childhood had been in Edinburgh, that there were other people's Edinburghs quite different from hers, and with which she held only the names of districts and streets and monuments in common. Similarly, there were other people's nineteen-thirties. So that, in her middle age, when she was at last allowed all those visitors to the convent – so many visitors being against the Rule, but a special dispensation was enforced on Sandy because of her Treatise – when a man said, 'I must have been at school in Edinburgh at the same time as you,

Sister Helena,' Sandy, who was now some years Sister Helena of the Transfiguration, clutched the bars of the grille as was her way, and peered at him through her little faint eyes and asked him to describe his schooldays and his school, and the Edinburgh he had known. And it turned out, once more, that his was a different Edinburgh from Sandy's. His school, where he was a boarder, had been cold and grey. His teachers had been supercilious Englishmen, 'or near-Englishmen', said the visitor 'with third-rate degrees'. Sandy could not remember ever having questioned the quality of her teachers' degrees, and the school had always been lit with the sun or, in winter, with a pearly north light. 'But Edinburgh,' said the man, 'was a beautiful city, more beautiful then than it is now. Of course, the slums have been cleared. The Old Town was always my favourite. We used to love to explore the Grassmarket and so on. Architecturally speaking, there is no finer sight in Europe.'

'I was once taken for a walk through the Canongate,' Sandy said, 'but I was frightened by the squalor.'

'Well, it was the 'thirties,' said the man. 'Tell me, Sister Helena, what would you say was your greatest influence during the 'thirties? I mean, during your teens. Did you read Auden and Eliot?'

'No,' said Sandy.

'We boys were very keen on Auden and that group of course. We wanted to go and fight in the Spanish Civil War. On the Republican side, of course. Did you take sides in the Spanish Civil War at your school?'

'Well, not exactly,' said Sandy. 'It was all different for us.'

'You weren't a Catholic then, of course?'

'No,' said Sandy.

'The influences of one's teens are very important,' said the man.

'Oh yes,' said Sandy, 'even if they provide something to react against.'

'What was your biggest influence, then, Sister Helena? Was it political, personal? Was it Calvinism?'

'Oh no,' said Sandy. 'But there was a Miss Jean Brodie in her prime.' She clutched the bars of the grille as if she wanted to escape from the dim parlour beyond, for she was not composed like the other nuns who sat, when they received their rare visitors, well back in the darkness with folded hands. But Sandy always leaned forward and peered, clutching the bars with both hands, and the other sisters remarked it and said that Sister Helena had too much to bear from the world since she had published her psychological book which was so unexpectedly famed. But the dispensation was forced upon Sandy, and she clutched the bars and received the choice visitors, the psychologists and the Catholic seekers, and the higher journalist ladies and the academics who wanted to question her about her odd psychological treatise on the nature of moral perception, called 'The Transfiguration of the Commonplace'.

'We will not go into St Giles',' said Miss Brodie, 'because the day draws late. But I presume you have all been to St Giles's Cathedral?'

They had nearly all been in St Giles' with its tattered blood-stained banners of the past. Sandy had not been there, and did not want to go. The outsides of old Edinburgh churches frightened her, they were of such dark stone, like presences almost the colour of the Castle rock, and were built so warningly with their upraised fingers.

Miss Brodie had shown them a picture of Cologne Cathedral, like a wedding cake, which looked as if it had been built for pleasure and festivities, and parties given by the Prodigal Son in his early career. But the insides of Scottish churches were more reassuring because during the services they contained people, and no ghosts at all. Sandy,

Rose Stanley and Monica Douglas were of believing though not church-going families. Jenny Gray and Mary Macgregor were Presbyterians and went to Sunday School. Eunice Gardiner was Episcopalian and claimed that she did not believe in Jesus, but in the Father, Son and Holy Ghost. Sandy, who believed in ghosts, felt that the Holy Ghost was a feasible proposition. The whole question was, during this winter term, being laid open by Miss Brodie who, at the same time as adhering to the strict Church of Scotland habits of her youth, and keeping the Sabbath, was now, in her prime, attending evening classes in comparative religion at the University. So her pupils heard all about it, and learned for the first time that some honest people did not believe in God, nor even Allah. But the girls were set to study the Gospels with diligence for their truth and goodness, and to read them aloud for their beauty.

Their walk had brought them into broad Chambers Street. The group had changed its order, and was now walking three abreast, with Miss Brodie in front between Sandy and Rose. 'I am summoned to see the headmistress at morning break on Monday,' said Miss Brodie. 'I have no doubt Miss Mackay wishes to question my methods of instruction. It has happened before. It will happen again. Meanwhile, I follow my principles of education and give of my best in my prime. The word "education" comes from the root *e* from *ex*, out, and *duco*, I lead. It means a leading out. To me education is a leading out of what is already there in the pupil's soul. To Miss Mackay it is a putting in of something that is not there, and that is not what I call education, I call it intrusion, from the Latin root prefix *in* meaning in and the stem *trudo*, I thrust. Miss Mackay's method is to thrust a lot of information into the pupil's head; mine is a leading out of knowledge, and that is true education as is proved by the root meaning. Now Miss Mackay has accused me of putting ideas into my girls' heads, but in fact that is *her* practice and mine is quite the opposite. Never let it be said that I put ideas into your heads. What is the meaning of education, Sandy?'

'To lead out,' said Sandy who was composing a formal invitation to Alan Breck, a year and a day after their breath-taking flight through the heather.

Miss Sandy Stranger requests the pleasure of Mr Alan Breck's company at dinner on Tuesday the 6th of January at 8 o'clock.

That would surprise the hero of *Kidnapped* coming unexpectedly from Sandy's new address in the lonely harbour house on the coast of Fife – described in a novel by the daughter of John Buchan – of which Sandy had now by devious means become the mistress. Alan Breck would arrive in full Highland dress. Supposing that passion struck upon them in the course of the evening and they were swept away into sexual intercourse? She saw the picture of it happening in her mind, and Sandy could not stand for this spoiling. She argued with herself, surely people have time to *think*, they have to stop to think while they are taking their clothes off, and if they stop to think, how can they be swept away?

'That is a Citroen,' said Rose Stanley about a motor car that had passed by. 'They are French.'

'Sandy, dear, don't rush. Take my hand,' said Miss Brodie. 'Rose, your mind is full of motor cars. There is nothing wrong with motor cars, of course, but there are higher things. I'm sure Sandy's mind is not on motor cars, she is paying attention to my conversation like a well-mannered girl.'

And if people take their clothes off in front of each other, thought Sandy, it is so rude, they are bound to be put off their passion for a moment. And if they are put off just for a single moment, *how* can they be swept away in the urge? If it all happens in a flash ...

Miss Brodie said, 'So I intend simply to point out to

37

Miss Mackay that there is a radical difference in our principles of education. Radical is a word pertaining to roots – Latin *radix*, a root. We differ at root, the headmistress and I, upon the question whether we are employed to educate the minds of girls or to intrude upon them. We have had this argument before, but Miss Mackay is not, I may say, an outstanding logician. A logician is one skilled in logic. Logic is the art of reasoning. What is logic, Rose?'

'To do with reasoning, ma'am,' said Rose, who later, while still in her teens, was to provoke Miss Brodie's amazement and then her awe and finally her abounding enthusiasm for the role which Rose then appeared to be enacting: that of a great lover, magnificently elevated above the ordinary run of lovers, above the moral laws, Venus incarnate, something set apart. In fact, Rose was not at the time in question engaged in the love affair which Miss Brodie thought she was, but it seemed so, and Rose was famous for sex. But in her mere eleventh year, on the winter's walk, Rose was taking note of the motor cars and Miss Brodie had not yet advanced far enough into her prime to speak of sex except by veiled allusion, as when she said of her warrior lover, 'He was a pure man', or when she read from James Hogg's poem 'Bonnie Kilmeny',

'Kilmeny was pure as pure could be'

and added, 'Which is to say, she did not go to the glen in order to mix with men.'

'When I see Miss Mackay on Monday morning,' said Miss Brodie, 'I shall point out that by the terms of my employment my methods cannot be condemned unless they can be proved to be in any part improper or subversive, and so long as the girls are in the least equipped for the end-of-term examination. I trust you girls to work hard and try and scrape through, even if you learn up the stuff and forget it next day. As for impropriety, it could never be imputed to me except by some gross distortion on the part of a traitor. I do not think ever to be betrayed. Miss Mackay is younger than I am and higher salaried. That is by accident. The best qualifications available at the University in my time were inferior to those open to Miss Mackay. That is why she holds the senior position. But her reasoning power is deficient, and so I have no fears for Monday.'

'Miss Mackay has an awfully red face, with the veins all showing,' said Rose.

'I can't permit that type of remark to pass in my presence, Rose,' said Miss Brodie, 'for it would be disloyal.'

They had come to the end of Lauriston Place, past the fire station, where they were to get on a tram-car to go to tea with Miss Brodie in her flat at Churchhill. A very long queue of men lined this part of the street. They were without collars, in shabby suits. They were talking and spitting and smoking little bits of cigarette held between middle finger and thumb.

'We shall cross here,' said Miss Brodie and herded the set across the road.

Monica Douglas whispered, 'They are the Idle.'

'In England they are called the Unemployed. They are waiting to get their dole from the labour bureau,' said Miss Brodie. 'You must all pray for the Unemployed, I will write you out the special prayer for them. You all know what the dole is?'

Eunice Gardiner had not heard of it.

'It is the weekly payment made by the State for the relief of the Unemployed and their families. Sometimes they go and spend their dole on drink before they go home, and their children starve. They are our brothers. Sandy, stop staring at once. In Italy the unemployment problem has been solved.'

Sandy felt that she was not staring across the road at the endless queue of brothers, but that it was pulling her eyes towards it. She felt once more very frightened. Some of the men looked over at the girls, but without seeing them. The girls had reached the tram stop. The men were talking and spitting a great deal. Some were laughing with hacking laughs merging into coughs and ending up with spits.

As they waited for the tram-car Miss Brodie said, 'I had lodgings in this street when first I came to Edinburgh as a student. I must tell you a story about the landlady, who was very frugal. It was her habit to come to me every morning to ask what I would have for breakfast, and she spoke like this: "Wud ye have a red herrin? – no ye wouldn't. Could ye eat a boilt egg? – no ye couldn't." The result was, I never had but bread and butter to my breakfast all the time I was in those lodgings, and very little of that.'

The laughter of the girls met that of the men opposite, who had now begun to file slowly by fits and starts into the labour bureau. Sandy's fear returned as soon as she had stopped laughing. She saw the slow jerkily moving file tremble with life, she saw it all of a piece like one dragon's body which had no right to be in the city and yet would not go away and was unslayable. She thought of the starving children. This was a relief to her fear. She wanted to cry as she always did when she saw a street singer or a beggar. She wanted Jenny to be there, because Jenny cried easily about poor children. But the snaky creature opposite started to shiver in the cold and made Sandy tremble again. She turned and said to Mary Macgregor who had brushed against her sleeve, 'Stop pushing.'

'Mary, dear, you mustn't push,' said Miss Brodie.

'I wasn't pushing,' said Mary.

In the tram-car Sandy excused herself from tea with Miss Brodie on the plea that she thought she had a cold coming on. Indeed she shivered. She wanted at that moment to be warmly at home, outside which even the corporate Brodie set lived in a colder sort of way.

But later, when Sandy thought of Eunice doing somersaults and splits on Miss Brodie's kitchen linoleum while the other girls washed up, she rather wished she had gone to tea at Miss Brodie's after all. She took out her secret notebook from between the sheets of music and added a chapter to 'The Mountain Eyrie', the true love story of Miss Jean Brodie.

Chapter Three

The days passed and the wind blew from the Forth.

It is not to be supposed that Miss Brodie was unique at this point of her prime; or that (since such things are relative) she was in any way off her head, She was alone, merely, in that she taught in a school like Marcia Blaine's. There were legions of her kind during the nineteen-thirties, women from the age of thirty and upward, who crowded their war-bereaved spinsterhood with voyages of discovery into new ideas and energetic practices in art or social welfare, education or religion. The progressive spinsters of Edinburgh did not teach in schools, especially in schools of traditional character like Marcia Blaine's School for Girls. It was in this that Miss Brodie was, as the rest of the staff spinsterhood put it, a trifle out of place. But she was not out of place amongst her own kind, the vigorous daughters of dead or enfeebled merchants, of ministers of religion, University professors, doctors, big warehouse owners of the past, or the owners of fisheries who had endowed these daughters with shrewd wits, high-coloured cheeks, constitutions like horses, logical educations, hearty spirits and private means. They could be seen leaning over the democratic counters of Edinburgh grocers' shops arguing with the Manager at three in the afternoon on every subject from the authenticity of the Scriptures to the question what the word 'guaranteed' on a jam-jar really meant. They went to lectures, tried living on honey and nuts, took lessons in German and then went walking in Germany; they bought caravans and went off with them into the hills among the lochs; they played the guitar, they supported all the new little theatre companies; they took lodgings in the slums and, distributing pots of paint, taught their neighbours the arts of simple interior decoration; they preached the inventions of Marie Stopes; they attended the meetings of the Oxford Group and put Spiritualism to their hawk-eyed test. Some assisted in the Scottish Nationalist Movement; others, like Miss Brodie, called themselves Europeans and Edinburgh a European capital, the city of Hume and Boswell.

They were not, however, committee women. They were not school-teachers. The committee spinsters were less enterprising and not at all rebellious, they were sober churchgoers and quiet workers. The school-mistresses were of a still more orderly type, earning their keep, living with aged parents and taking walks on the hills and holidays at North Berwick.

But those of Miss Brodie's kind were great talkers and feminists and, like most feminists, talked to men as man-to-man.

'I tell you this, Mr Geddes, birth control is the only answer to the problem of the working class. A free issue to every household ...'

And often in the thriving grocers' shops at three in the afternoon:

'Mr Logan, Elder though you are, I am a woman in my prime of life, so you can take it from me that you get a sight more religion out of Professor Tovey's Sunday concerts than you do out of your kirk services.'

And so, seen in this light, there was nothing outwardly odd about Miss Brodie. Inwardly was a different matter, and it remained to be seen, towards what extremities her nature worked her. Outwardly she differed from the rest of the teaching staff in that she was still in a state of fluctuating development, whereas they had only too understandably not trusted themselves to change their minds, particularly on ethical questions, after the age of twenty. There was nothing Miss Brodie could not yet learn, she boasted of it. And it was not a static Miss Brodie who told her girls,

43

'These are the years of my prime. You are benefiting by my prime', but one whose nature was growing under their eyes, as the girls themselves were under formation. It extended, this prime of Miss Brodie's, still in the making when the girls were well on in their teens. And the principles governing the end of her prime would have astonished herself at the beginning of it.

The summer holidays of nineteen-thirty-one marked the first anniversary of the launching of Miss Brodie's prime. The year to come was in many ways the sexual year of the Brodie set, who were now turned eleven and twelve: it was a crowded year of stirring revelations. In later years, sex was only one of the things in life. That year it was everything.

The term opened vigorously as usual. Miss Brodie stood bronzed before her class and said, 'I have spent most of my summer holidays in Italy once more, and a week in London, and I have brought back a great many pictures which we can pin on the wall. Here is a Cimabue. Here is a larger formation of Mussolini's fascisti, it is a better view of them than that of last year's picture. They are doing splendid things as I shall tell you later. I went with my friends for an audience with the Pope. My friends kissed his ring but I thought it proper only to bend over it. I wore a long black gown with a lace mantilla, and looked magnificent. In London my friends who are well-to-do – their small girl has two nurses, or nannies as they say in England – took me to visit A. A. Milne. In the hall was hung a reproduction of Botticelli's *Primavera* which means the Birth of Spring. I wore my silk dress with the large red poppies which is just right for my colouring. Mussolini is one of the greatest men in the world, far more so than Ramsay MacDonald, and his fascisti –'

'Good morning, Miss Brodie. Good morning, sit down, girls,' said the headmistress who had entered in a hurry, leaving the door wide open.

44

Miss Brodie passed behind her with her head up, up, and shut the door with the utmost meaning.

'I have only just looked in,' said Miss Mackay, 'and I have to be off. Well, girls, this is the first day of the new session. Are we downhearted? No. You girls must work hard this year at every subject and pass your qualifying examination with flying colours. Next year you will be in the Senior school, remember. I hope you've all had a nice summer holiday, you all look nice and brown. I hope in due course of time to read your essays on how you spent them.'

When she had gone Miss Brodie looked hard at the door for a long time. A girl, not of her set, called Judith, giggled. Miss Brodie said to Judith, ''That will do.' She turned to the blackboard and rubbed out with her duster the long division sum she always kept on the blackboard in case of intrusions from outside during any arithmetic periods when Miss Brodie should happen not to be teaching arithmetic. When she had done this she turned back to the class and said, 'Are we downhearted no, are we downhearted no. As I was saying, Mussolini has performed feats of magnitude and unemployment is even farther abolished under him than it was last year. I shall be able to tell you a great deal this term. As you know, I don't believe in talking down to children, you are capable of grasping more than is generally appreciated by your elders. Education means a leading out, from *e*, out and *duco*, I lead. Qualifying examination or no qualifying examination, you will have the benefit of my experiences in Italy. In Rome I saw the Forum and I saw the Colosseum where the gladiators died and the slaves were thrown to the lions. A vulgar American remarked to me, "It looks like a mighty fine quarry." They talk nasally. Mary, what does to talk nasally mean?'

Mary did not know.

'Stupid as ever,' said Miss Brodie. 'Eunice?'

'Through your nose,' said Eunice.

'Answer in a complete sentence, please,' said Miss Brodie.

'This year I think you should all start answering in complete sentences, I must try to remember this rule. Your correct answer is "To talk nasally means to talk through one's nose". The American said, "It looks like a mighty fine quarry." Ah, It was there the gladiators fought. "Hail Caesar!" they cried. "These about to die salute thee!"'

Miss Brodie stood in her brown dress like a gladiator with raised arm and eyes flashing like a sword. 'Hail Caesar!' she cried again, turning radiantly to the window light, as if Caesar sat there. 'Who opened the window?' said Miss Brodie dropping her arm.

Nobody answered.

'Whoever has opened the window has opened it too wide,' said Miss Brodie. 'Six inches is perfectly adequate. More is vulgar. One should have an innate sense of these things. We ought to be doing history at the moment according to the time-table. Get out your history books and prop them up in your hands. I shall tell you a little more about Italy. I met a young poet by a fountain. Here is a picture of Dante meeting Beatrice – it is pronounced Beatri*chay* in Italian which makes the name very beautiful – on the Ponte Vecchio. He fell in love with her at that moment. Mary, sit up and don't slouch. It was a sublime moment in a sublime love. By whom was the picture painted?'

Nobody knew.

'It was painted by Rossetti. Who was Rossetti, Jenny?'

'A painter,' said Jenny.

Miss Brodie looked suspicious.

'And a genius,' said Sandy, to come to Jenny's rescue.

'A friend of – ?' said Miss Brodie.

'Swinburne,' said a girl.

Miss Brodie smiled. 'You have not forgotten,' she said, looking round the class. 'Holidays or no holidays. Keep your history books propped up in case we have any further intruders.' She looked disapprovingly towards the door and lifted her fine dark Roman head with dignity. She had often told the girls that her dead Hugh had admired her head for its Roman appearance.

'Next year,' she said, 'you will have the specialists to teach you history and mathematics and languages, a teacher for this and a teacher for that, a period of forty-five minutes for this and another for that. But in this your last year with me you will receive the fruits of my prime. They will remain with you all your days. First, however, I must mark the register for today before we forget. There are two new girls. Stand up the two new girls.'

They stood up with wide eyes while Miss Brodie sat down at her desk.

'You will get used to our ways. What religions are you?' said Miss Brodie with her pen poised on the page while, outside in the sky, the gulls from the Firth of Forth wheeled over the school and the green and golden tree-tops swayed towards the windows.

> 'Come autumn sae pensive, in yellow and gray,
> And soothe me wi' tidings o' nature's decay

– Robert Burns,' said Miss Brodie when she had closed the register. 'We are now well into the nineteen-thirties. I have four pounds of rosy apples in my desk, a gift from Mr Lowther's orchard, let us eat them now while the coast is clear – not but what the apples do not come under my own jurisdiction, but discretion is . . . discretion is . . . Sandy?'

'The better part of valour, Miss Brodie.' Her little eyes looked at Miss Brodie in a slightly smaller way.

Even before the official opening of her prime Miss Brodie's colleagues in the Junior school had been gradually turning against her. The teaching staff of the Senior school was indifferent or mildly amused, for they had not yet felt the impact of the Brodie set; that was to come the following year, and even then these senior mistresses were not unduly irritated by the effects of what they called Miss Brodie's experimental methods. It was in the Junior school, among the lesser paid and lesser qualified women, with whom Miss Brodie had daily dealings, that indignation seethed. There were two exceptions on the staff, who felt neither resentment nor indifference towards Miss Brodie, but were, on the contrary, her supporters on every count. One of these was Mr Gordon Lowther, the singing master for the whole school, Junior and Senior. The other was Mr Teddy Lloyd, the Senior girls' art master. They were the only men on the staff. Both were already a little in love with Miss Brodie, for they found in her the only sex-bestirred object in their daily environment, and although they did not realize it, both were already beginning to act as rivals for her attention. But so far, they had not engaged her attention as men, she knew them only as supporters, and was proudly grateful. It was the Brodie set who discerned, before she did, and certainly these men did, that Mr Lowther and Mr Lloyd were at pains to appear well, each in his exclusive right before Miss Brodie.

To the Brodie set Gordon Lowther and Teddy Lloyd looked rather like each other until habitual acquaintance proved that they looked very different. Both were red-gold in colouring. Teddy Lloyd, the art master, was by far the better-shaped, the better-featured and the more sophisticated. He was said to be half Welsh, half English. He spoke with a hoarse voice as if he had bronchitis all the time. A golden forelock of his hair fell over his forehead into his eyes. Most wonderful of all, he had only one arm, the right, with which he painted. The other was a sleeve tucked into his pocket. He had lost the contents of the sleeve in the Great War.

Miss Brodie's class had only once had an opportunity to size him up closely, and then it was in a dimmed light, for the blinds of the art room had been drawn to allow Mr Lloyd to show his lantern slides. They had been marched into the art room by Miss Brodie, who was going to sit with the girls on the end of a bench, when the art master came forward with a chair for her held in his one hand and presented in a special way with a tiny inflection of the knees, like a flunkey. Miss Brodie seated herself nobly like Britannia with her legs apart under her loose brown skirt which came well over her knees. Mr Lloyd showed his pictures from an exhibition of Italian art in London. He had a pointer with which he indicated the design of the picture in accompaniment to his hoarse voice. He said nothing of what the pictures represented, only followed each curve and line as the artist had left it off – perhaps at the point of an elbow – and picked it up – perhaps at the edge of a cloud or the back of a chair. The ladies of the *Primavera*, in their netball-playing postures, provided Mr Lloyd with much pointer work. He kept on passing the pointer along the lines of their bottoms which showed through the drapery. The third time he did this a collective quiver of mirth ran along the front row of girls, then spread to the back rows. They kept their mouths shut tight against these convulsions, but the tighter their lips, the more did the little gusts of humour escape through their noses. Mr Lloyd looked round with offended exasperation.

'It is obvious,' said Miss Brodie, 'that these girls are not of cultured homes and heritage. The Philistines are upon us, Mr Lloyd.'

The girls, anxious to be of cultured and sexless antecedents, were instantly composed by the shock of this remark. But immediately Mr Lloyd resumed his demonstration of artistic form, and again dragged his pointer all round the draped private parts of one of Botticelli's female subjects, Sandy affected to have a fit of spluttering coughs, as did several girls behind her. Others groped under their seat as if looking for something they had dropped. One or two frankly leant against each other and giggled with hands to their helpless mouths.

'I am surprised at *you*, Sandy,' said Miss Brodie. 'I thought you were the leaven in the lump.'

Sandy looked up from her coughs with a hypocritical blinking of her eyes. Miss Brodie, however, had already fastened on Mary Macgregor who was nearest to her. Mary's giggles had been caused by contagion, for she was too stupid to have any sex-wits of her own, and Mr Lloyd's lesson would never have affected her unless it had first affected the rest of the class. But now she was giggling openly like a dirty-minded child of an uncultured home. Miss Brodie grasped Mary's arm, jerked her to her feet and propelled her to the door where she thrust her outside and shut her out, returning as one who had solved the whole problem. As indeed she had, for the violent action sobered the girls and made them feel that, in the official sense, an unwanted ring-leader had been apprehended and they were no longer in the wrong.

As Mr Lloyd had now switched his equipment to a depiction of the Madonna and Child, Miss Brodie's action was the more appreciated, for no one in the class would have felt comfortable at being seized with giggles while Mr Lloyd's pointer was tracing the outlines of this sacred subject. In fact, they were rather shocked that Mr Lloyd's hoarse voice did not change its tone in the slightest for this occasion, but went on stating what the painter had done with his brush; he was almost defiant in his methodical tracing of lines all over the Mother and the Son. Sandy caught his glance towards Miss Brodie as if seeking her approval for his very artistic attitude and Sandy saw her smile back as would a goddess with superior understanding smile to a god away on the mountain tops.

It was not long after this that Monica Douglas, later famous for mathematics and anger, claimed that she had seen Mr Lloyd in the act of kissing Miss Brodie. She was very definite about it in her report to the five other members of the Brodie set. There was a general excited difficulty in believing her.

'When?'

'Where?'

'In the art room after school yesterday.'

'What were you doing in the art room?' said Sandy who took up the role of cross-examiner.

'I went to get a new sketch pad.'

'Why? You haven't finished your old sketch pad yet.'

'I have,' said Monica.

'When did you use up your old sketch pad?'

'Last Saturday afternoon when you were playing golf with Miss Brodie.'

It was true that Jenny and Sandy had done nine holes on the Braid Hills course with Miss Brodie on the previous Saturday, while the rest of the Brodie set wandered afield to sketch.

'Monica used up all her book. She did the Tee Woods from five angles,' said Rose Stanley in verification.

'What part of the art room were they standing in?' Sandy said.

'The far side,' Monica said. 'I know he had his arm round her and was kissing her. They jumped apart when I opened the door.'

'Which arm?' Sandy snapped.

'The right of course, he hasn't got a left.'

'Were you inside or outside the room when you saw them?' Sandy said.

'Well, in and out. I *saw* them, I tell you.'

'What did they say?' Jenny said.

'They didn't see me,' said Monica. 'I just turned and ran away.'

'Was it a long and lingering kiss?' Sandy demanded, while Jenny came closer to hear the answer.

Monica cast the corner of her eye up to the ceiling as if

doing mental arithmetic. Then when her calculation was finished she said, 'Yes it was.'

'How do you know if you didn't stop to see how long it was?'

'I know,' said Monica, getting angry, 'by the bit that I did see. It was a small bit of a good long kiss that I saw, I could tell it by his arm being round her, and –'

'I don't believe all this,' Sandy said squeakily, because she was excited and desperately trying to prove the report true by eliminating the doubts. 'You must have been dreaming,' she said.

Monica pecked with the fingers of her right hand at Sandy's arm, and pinched the skin of it with a nasty half turn. Sandy screamed. Monica, whose face was becoming very red, swung the attaché case which held her books, so that it hit the girls who stood in its path and made them stand back from her.

'She's losing her temper,' said Eunice Gardiner, skipping.

'I don't believe what she says,' said Sandy, desperately trying to visualize the scene in the art room and to goad factual Monica into describing it with due feeling.

'I believe it,' said Rose. 'Mr Lloyd is an artist and Miss Brodie is artistic too.'

Jenny said, 'Didn't they see the door opening?'

'Yes,' said Monica, 'they jumped apart as I opened the door.'

'How did you know they didn't see you?' Sandy said.

'I got away before they turned round. They were standing at the far end of the room beside the still-life curtain.' She went to the classroom door and demonstrated her quick get-away. This was not dramatically satisfying to Sandy who went out of the classroom, opened the door, looked, opened her eyes in a startled way, gasped and retreated in a flash. She seemed satisfied by her experimental re-enactment but it so delighted her friends that she repeated it. Miss

Brodie came up from behind her on her fourth performance which had reached a state of extreme flourish.

'What are you doing, Sandy?' said Miss Brodie.

'Only playing,' said Sandy, photographing this new Miss Brodie with her little eyes.

The question of whether Miss Brodie was actually capable of being kissed and of kissing occupied the Brodie set till Christmas. For the war-time romance of her life had presented to their minds a Miss Brodie of hardly flesh and blood, since that younger Miss Brodie belonged to the prehistory of before their birth. Sitting under the elm last autumn, Miss Brodie's story of 'when I was a girl' had seemed much less real, and yet more believable than this report by Monica Douglas. The Brodie set decided to keep the incident to themselves lest, if it should spread to the rest of the class, it should spread wider still and eventually to someone's ears who would get Monica Douglas into trouble.

There was, indeed, a change in Miss Brodie. It was not merely that Sandy and Jenny, recasting her in their minds, now began to try to imagine her as someone called 'Jean'. There was a change in herself. She wore newer clothes and with them a glowing amber necklace which was of such real amber that, as she once showed them, it had magnetic properties when rubbed and then applied to a piece of paper.

The change in Miss Brodie was best discerned by comparison with the other teachers in the Junior school. If you looked at them and then looked at Miss Brodie it was more possible to imagine her giving herself up to kissing.

Jenny and Sandy wondered if Mr Lloyd and Miss Brodie had gone further that day in the art room, and had been swept away by passion. They kept an eye on Miss Brodie's stomach to see if it showed signs of swelling. Some days, if they were bored, they decided it had begun to swell. But on Miss Brodie's entertaining days they found her stomach is flat as ever and at these times even agreed together that Monica Douglas had been telling a lie.

The other Junior school teachers said good morning to Miss Brodie, these days, in a more than Edinburgh manner, that is to say it was gracious enough, and not one of them omitted to say good morning at all; but Sandy, who had turned eleven, perceived that the tone of 'morning' in good morning made the word seem purposely to rhyme with 'scorning', so that these colleagues of Miss Brodie's might just as well have said 'I scorn you' instead of good morning. Miss Brodie's reply was more than ever anglicized in its accent than was its usual proud wont. 'Good mawning,' she replied, in the corridors, flattening their scorn beneath the chariot wheels of her superiority, and deviating her head towards them no more than an insulting half-inch. She held her head up, up, as she walked, and often, when she reached and entered her own classroom, permitted herself to sag gratefully against the door for an instant. She did not frequent the staff common rooms in the free periods when her class was taking its singing or sewing lessons, but accompanied them.

Now the two sewing teachers were somewhat apart from the rest of the teaching staff and were not taken seriously. They were the two younger sisters of a third, dead, eldest sister whose guidance of their lives had never been replaced. Their names were Miss Ellen and Miss Alison Kerr; they were incapable of imparting any information whatsoever, so flustered were they, with their fluffed-out hair, dry blue-grey skins and birds' eyes; instead of teaching sewing they took each girl's work in hand, one by one, and did most of it for her. In the worst cases they unstitched what had been done and did it again, saying 'This'll not do', or 'That's never a run and fell seam'. The sewing sisters had not as yet been induced to judge Miss Brodie since they were by nature of the belief that their scholastic colleagues were above criticism. Therefore the sewing lessons were a great relaxation to all, and Miss Brodie in the time before Christmas used the sewing period each week to read *Jane Eyre* to her class who, while they listened, pricked their thumbs as much as was bearable so that interesting little spots of blood might appear on the stuff they were sewing, and it was even possible to make blood-spot designs.

The singing lessons were far different. Some weeks after the report of her kissing in the art room it gradually became plain that Miss Brodie was agitated before, during, and after the singing lessons. She wore her newest clothes on singing days.

Sandy said to Monica Douglas, 'Are you sure it was Mr Lloyd who kissed her? Are you sure it wasn't Mr Lowther?'

'It was Mr Lloyd,' said Monica, 'and it was in the art room, not the music room. What would Mr Lowther have been doing in the art room?'

'They look alike, Mr Lloyd and Mr Lowther,' Sandy said.

Monica's anger was rising in her face. 'It was Mr Lloyd with his one arm round her,' she said. 'I saw them. I'm sorry I ever told you. Rose is the only one that believes me.'

Rose Stanley believed her, but this was because she was indifferent. She was the least of all the Brodie set to be excited by Miss Brodie's love affairs, or by anyone else's sex. And it was always to be the same. Later, when she was famous for sex, her magnificently appealing qualities lay in the fact that she had no curiosity about sex at all, she never reflected upon it. As Miss Brodie was to say, she had instinct.

'Rose is the only one who believes me,' said Monica Douglas.

When she visited Sandy at the nunnery in the late nineteen-fifties, Monica said, 'I really did see Teddy Lloyd kiss Miss Brodie in the art room one day.'

'I know you did,' said Sandy.

She knew it even before Miss Brodie had told her so one day after the end of the war, when they sat in the Braid

Hills Hotel eating sandwiches and drinking tea which Miss Brodie's rations at home would not run to. Miss Brodie sat shrivelled and betrayed in her long-preserved dark mus-quash coat. She had been retired before time. She said, 'I am past my prime.'

'It was a good prime,' said Sandy.

They looked out of the wide windows at the little Braid Burn trickling through the fields and at the hills beyond, so austere from everlasting that they had never been capable of losing anything by the war.

'Teddy Lloyd was greatly in love with me, as you know,' said Miss Brodie, 'and I with him. It was a great love. One day in the art room he kissed me. We never became lovers, not even after you left Edinburgh, when the temptation was strongest.'

Sandy stared through her little eyes at the hills.

'But I renounced him,' said Miss Brodie. 'He was a married man. I renounced the great love of my prime. We had everything in common, the artistic nature.'

She had reckoned on her prime lasting till she was sixty. But this, the year after the war, was in fact Miss Brodie's last and fifty-sixth year. She looked older than that, she was suffering from an internal growth. This was her last year in the world and in another sense it was Sandy's.

Miss Brodie sat in her defeat and said, 'In the late autumn of nineteen thirty-one – are you listening, Sandy?'

Sandy took her eyes from the hills.

In the late autumn of nineteen-thirty-one Miss Brodie was away from school for two weeks. It was understood she had an ailment. The Brodie set called at her flat after school with flowers and found no one at home. On inquiring at school next day they were told she had gone to the coun-try to stay with a friend until she was better.

In the meantime Miss Brodie's class was dispersed, and squashed in among the classes of her colleagues. The Brodie set stuck together and were placed with a gaunt woman who was, in fact, a Miss Gaunt from the Western Isles who wore a knee-length skirt made from what looked like grey blanket stuff; this had never been smart even in the knee-length days; Rose Stanley said it was cut short for economy. Her head was very large and bony. Her chest was a slight bulge flattened by a bust bodice, and her jersey was a dark forbidding green. She did not care at all for the Brodie set who were stunned by a sudden plunge into industrious learning and very put out by Miss Gaunt's horrible sharpness and strict insistence on silence throughout the day.

'Oh dear,' said Rose out loud one day when they were settled to essay writing, 'I can't remember how you spell "possession". Are there two 's's or –?'

'A hundred lines of *Marmion*,' Miss Gaunt flung at her.

The black-marks book which eventually reflected itself on the end-of-term reports, was heavily scored with the names of the Brodie set by the end of the first week. Apart from inquiring their names for this purpose Miss Gaunt did not trouble to remember them. 'You, girl,' she would say to every Brodie face. So dazed were the Brodie girls that they did not notice the omission during that week of their singing lesson which should have been on Wednesday.

On Thursday they were herded into the sewing room in the early afternoon. The two sewing teachers, Miss Alison and Miss Ellen Kerr, seemed rather cowed by gaunt Miss Gaunt, and applied themselves briskly to the sewing machines which they were teaching the girls to use. The shuttle of the sewing machines went up and down, which usually caused Sandy and Jenny to giggle, since at that time everything that could conceivably bear a sexual interpretation immediately did so to them. But the absence of Miss Brodie and the presence of Miss Gaunt had a definite subtracting effect from the sexual significance of everything, and the trepidation of the two sewing sisters contributed to the effect of grim realism.

Miss Gaunt evidently went to the same parish church as

the Kerr sisters, to whom she addressed remarks from time to time while she embroidered a tray cloth.

'My brothurr ...' she kept saying, 'my brothurr says ...'

Miss Gaunt's brother was apparently the minister of the parish, which accounted for the extra precautions Miss Alison and Miss Ellen were taking about their work today, with the result that they got a lot of the sewing mixed up.

'My brothurr is up in the morning at five-thirty ... My brothurr organized a ...'

Sandy was thinking of the next instalment of *Jane Eyre* which Miss Brodie usually enlivened this hour by reading. Sandy had done with Alan Breck and had taken up with Mr Rochester, with whom she now sat in the garden.

'You are afraid of me, Miss Sandy.'

'You talk like the Sphinx, sir, but I am not afraid.'

'You have such a grave, quiet manner, Miss Sandy – you are going?'

'It has struck nine, sir.'

A phrase of Miss Gaunt's broke upon the garden scene: 'Mr Lowther is not at school this week.'

'So I hear,' Miss Alison said.

'It seems he will be away for another week at least.'

'Is he ill?'

'I understand so, unfortunately,' said Miss Gaunt.

'Miss Brodie is ailing, too,' said Miss Ellen.

'Yes,' said Miss Gaunt. 'She too is expected to be absent for another week.'

'What is the trouble?'

'That I couldn't say,' said Miss Gaunt. She stuck her needle in and out of her embroidery. Then she looked up at the sisters. 'It may be Miss Brodie has the same complaint as Mr Lowther,' she said.

Sandy saw her face as that of the housekeeper in *Jane Eyre*, watching her carefully and knowingly as she entered the house, late, from the garden where she had been sitting with Mr Rochester.

'Perhaps Miss Brodie is having a love affair with Mr Lowther,' Sandy said to Jenny, merely in order to break up the sexless gloom that surrounded them.

'But it was Mr Lloyd who kissed her. She must be in love with Mr Lloyd or she wouldn't have let him kiss her.'

'Perhaps she's working it off on Mr Lowther. Mr Lowther isn't married.'

It was a fantasy worked up between them, in defiance of Miss Gaunt and her forbidding brother, and it was understood in that way. But Sandy, remembering Miss Gaunt's expression as she remarked 'It may be Miss Brodie has the same complaint as Mr Lowther', was suddenly not sure that the suggestion was not true. For this reason she was more reticent than Jenny about the details of the imagined love affair. Jenny whispered, 'They go to bed. Then he puts out the light. Then their toes touch. And then Miss Brodie ... Miss Brodie ...' She broke into giggles.

'Miss Brodie yawns,' said Sandy in order to restore decency, now that she suspected it was all true.

'No, Miss Brodie says "Darling". She says –'

'Quiet,' whispered Sandy, 'Eunice is coming.'

Eunice Gardiner approached the table where Jenny and Sandy sat, grabbed the scissors and went away. Eunice had lately taken a religious turn and there was no talking about sex in front of her. She had stopped hopping and skipping. The phase did not last long, but while it did she was nasty and not to be trusted. When she was well out of the way Jenny resumed:

'Mr Lowther's legs are shorter than Miss Brodie's, so I suppose she winds hers round his, and –'

'Where does Mr Lowther live, do you know?' Sandy said.

'At Cramond. He's got a big house with a housekeeper.'

In that year after the war when Sandy sat with Miss

Brodie in the window of the Braid Hills Hotel and brought her eyes back from the hills to show she was listening, Miss Brodie said:

'I renounced Teddy Lloyd. But I decided to enter into a love affair, it was the only cure. My love for Teddy was an obsession, he was the love of my prime. But in the autumn of nineteen-thirty-one I entered an affair with Gordon Lowther, he was a bachelor and it was more becoming. That is the truth and there is no more to say. Are you listening, Sandy?'

'Yes, I'm listening.'

'You look as if you were thinking of something else, my dear. Well, as I say, that is the whole story.'

Sandy was thinking of something else. She was thinking that it was not the whole story.

'Of course the liaison was suspected. Perhaps you girls knew about it. You, Sandy, had a faint idea . . . but nobody could prove what was between Gordon Lowther and myself. It was never proved. It was not on those grounds that I was betrayed. I should like to know who betrayed me. It is incredible that it should have been one of my own girls. I often wonder if it was poor Mary. Perhaps I should have been nicer to Mary. Well, it was tragic about Mary, I picture that fire, that poor girl. I can't see how Mary could have betrayed me, though.'

'She had no contact with the school after she left,' Sandy said.

'I wonder, was it Rose who betrayed me?'

The whine in her voice – '. . . betrayed me, betrayed me' – bored and afflicted Sandy. It is seven years, thought Sandy, since I betrayed this tiresome woman. What does she mean by 'betray'? She was looking at the hills as if to see there the first and unbetrayable Miss Brodie, indifferent to criticism as a crag.

After her two weeks' absence Miss Brodie returned to tell

her class that she had enjoyed an exciting rest and a well-earned one. Mr Lowther's singing class went on as usual and he beamed at Miss Brodie as she brought them proudly into the music room with their heads up, up. Miss Brodie now played the accompaniment, sitting very well at the piano and sometimes, with a certain sadness of countenance, richly taking the second soprano in 'How sweet is the shepherd's sweet lot', and other melodious preparations for the annual concert. Mr Lowther, short-legged, shy and golden-haired, no longer played with Jenny's curls. The bare branches brushed the windows and Sandy was almost as sure as could be that the singing master was in love with Miss Brodie and that Miss Brodie was in love with the art master. Rose Stanley had not yet revealed her potentialities in the working-out of Miss Brodie's passion for one-armed Teddy Lloyd, and Miss Brodie's prime still flourished unbetrayed.

It was impossible to imagine Miss Brodie sleeping with Mr Lowther, it was impossible to imagine her in a sexual context at all, and yet it was impossible not to suspect that such things were so.

During the Easter term Miss Mackay, the headmistress, had the girls in to tea in her study in small groups and, later, one by one. This was a routine of inquiry as to their intentions for the Senior School, whether they would go on the Modern side or whether they would apply for admission to the Classic l.

Miss Brodie had already prompted them as follows: ' I am not saying anything against the Modern side. Modern and Classical, they are equal, and each provides for a function in life. You must make your free choice. Not everyone is capable of a Classical education. You must make your choice quite freely.' So that the girls were left in no doubt as to Miss Brodie's contempt for the Modern side.

From among her special set only Eunice Gardiner stood out to be a Modern, and that was because her parents wanted her to take a course in domestic science and she herself wanted the extra scope for gymnastics and games which the Modern side offered. Eunice, preparing arduously for Confirmation, was still a bit too pious for Miss Brodie's liking. She now refused to do somersaults outside of the gymnasium, she wore lavender water on her handkerchief, declined a try of Rose Stanley's aunt's lipstick, was taking a suspiciously healthy interest in international sport and, when Miss Brodie herded her set to the Empire Theatre for their first and last opportunity to witness the dancing of Pavlova, Eunice was absent, she had pleaded off because of something else she had to attend which she described as 'a social'.

'Social what?' said Miss Brodie, who always made difficulties about words when she scented heresy.

'It's in the Church Hall, Miss Brodie.'

'Yes, yes, but social what? Social is an adjective and you are using it as a noun. If you mean a social gathering, by all means attend your social gathering and we shall have our own social gathering in the presence of the great Anna Pavlova, a dedicated woman who, when she appears on the stage, makes the other dancers look like elephants. By all means attend your social gathering. We shall see Pavlova doing the death of the Swan, it is a great moment in eternity.'

All that term she tried to inspire Eunice to become at least a pioneer missionary in some deadly and dangerous zone of the earth, for it was intolerable to Miss Brodie that any of her girls should grow up not largely dedicated to some vocation. 'You will end up as a Girl Guide leader in a suburb like Corstorphine,' she said warningly to Eunice, who was in fact secretly attracted to this idea and who lived in Corstorphine. The term was filled with legends of Pavlova and her dedicated habits, her wild fits of temperament and her intolerance of the second-rate. 'She screams at the chorus,' said Miss Brodie, 'which is permissible in a great artist. She speaks English fluently, her accent is charming. Afterwards she goes home to meditate upon the swans which she keeps on a lake in the grounds.'

'Sandy,' said Anna Pavlova, 'you are the only truly dedicated dancer, next to me. Your dying Swan is perfect, such a sensitive, final tap of the claw upon the floor of the stage . . .'

'I know it,' said Sandy (in considered preference to 'Oh, I do my best'), as she relaxed in the wings.

Pavlova nodded sagely and gazed into the middle distance with the eyes of tragic exile and of art. 'Every artist knows,' said Pavlova, 'is it not so?' Then, with a voice desperate with the menace of hysteria, and a charming accent, she declared, 'I have never been understood. Never. Never.'

Sandy removed one of her ballet shoes and cast it casually to the other end of the wings where it was respectfully retrieved by a member of the common chorus. Pausing before she removed the other shoe, Sandy said to Pavlova, 'I am sure I understand you.'

'It is true,' exclaimed Pavlova, clasping Sandy's hand, 'because you are an artist and will carry on the torch.'

Miss Brodie said: 'Pavlova contemplates her swans in order to perfect her swan dance, she studies them. That is true dedication. You must all grow up to be dedicated women as I have dedicated myself to you.'

A few weeks before she died, when, sitting up in bed in the nursing home, she learnt from Monica Douglas that Sandy had gone to a convent, she said: 'What a waste. That is not the sort of dedication I meant. Do you think she has done this to annoy me? I begin to wonder if it was not Sandy who betrayed me.'

The headmistress invited Sandy, Jenny and Mary to tea just before the Easter holidays and asked them the usual questions about what they wanted to do in the Senior school and whether they wanted to do it on the Modern or the

Classical side. Mary Macgregor was ruled out of the Classical side because her marks did not reach the required standard. She seemed despondent on hearing this.

'Why do you want so much to go on the Classical side, Mary? You aren't cut out for it. Don't your parents realize that?'

'Miss Brodie prefers it.'

'It has nothing to do with Miss Brodie,' said Miss Mackay, settling her great behind more firmly in her chair. 'It is a question of your marks or what you and your parents think. In your case, your marks don't come up to the standard.'

When Jenny and Sandy opted for Classical, she said: 'Because Miss Brodie prefers it, I suppose. What good will Latin and Greek be to you when you get married or take a job? German would be more useful.'

But they stuck out for Classical, and when Miss Mackay had accepted their choice she transparently started to win over the girls by praising Miss Brodie. 'What we would do without Miss Brodie, I don't know. There is always a difference about Miss Brodie's girls, and the last two years I may say a *marked* difference.'

Then she began to pump them. Miss Brodie took them to the theatre, the art galleries, for walks, to Miss Brodie's flat for tea? How kind of Miss Brodie. 'Does Miss Brodie pay for all your theatre tickets?'

'Sometimes,' said Mary.

'Not for all of us every time,' said Jenny.

'We go up to the gallery,' Sandy said.

'Well, it is most kind of Miss Brodie. I hope you are appreciative.'

'Oh, yes,' they said, united and alert against anything unfavourable to the Brodie idea which the conversation might be leading up to. This was not lost on the headmistress.

'That's splendid,' she said. 'And do you go to concerts

with Miss Brodie? Miss Brodie is very musical, I believe?'

'Yes,' said Mary, looking at her friends for a lead.

'We went to the opera with Miss Brodie last term to see *La Traviata*,' said Jenny.

'Miss Brodie is musical?' said Miss Mackay again, addressing Sandy and Jenny.

'We saw Pavlova,' said Sandy.

'Miss Brodie is musical?' said Miss Mackay.

'I think Miss Brodie is more interested in art, ma'am,' said Sandy.

'But music is a form of art.'

'Pictures and drawings, I mean,' said Sandy.

'Very enlightening,' said Miss Mackay. 'Do you girls take piano lessons?'

They all said yes.

'From whom? From Mr Lowther?'

They answered variously, for Mr Lowther's piano lessons were not part of the curriculum and these three girls had private arrangements for the piano at home. But now, at the mention of Mr Lowther, even slow-minded Mary suspected what Miss Mackay was driving at.

'I understand Miss Brodie plays the piano for your singing lessons. So what makes you think she prefers art to music, Sandy?'

'Miss Brodie told us so. Music is an interest to her but art is a passion, Miss Brodie said.'

'And what are *your* cultural interests? I'm sure you are too young to have passions.'

'Stories, ma'am,' Mary said.

'Does Miss Brodie tell you stories?'

'Yes,' said Mary.

'What about?'

'History,' said Jenny and Sandy together, because it was a question they had foreseen might arise one day and they had prepared the answer with a brainracking care for literal truth.

Miss Mackay paused and looked at them in the process of moving the cake from the table to the tray; their reply had plainly struck her as being on the ready side.

She asked no further questions, but made the following noteworthy speech:

'You are very fortunate in Miss Brodie. I could wish your arithmetic papers had been better. I am always impressed by Miss Brodie's girls in one way or another. You will have to work hard at ordinary humble subjects for the qualifying examination. Miss Brodie is giving you an excellent preparation for the Senior school. Culture cannot compensate for lack of hard knowledge. I am happy to see you are devoted to Miss Brodie. Your loyalty is due to the school rather than to any one individual.'

Not all of this conversation was reported back to Miss Brodie.

'We told Miss Mackay how much you liked art,' said Sandy, however.

'I do indeed,' said Miss Brodie, 'but "like" is hardly the word; pictorial art is my passion.'

'That's what I said,' said Sandy.

Miss Brodie looked at her as if to say, as in fact she had said twice before, 'One day, Sandy, you will go too far for my liking.'

'Compared to music,' said Sandy, blinking up at her with her little pig-like eyes.

Towards the end of the Easter holidays, to crown the sex-laden year, Jenny, out walking alone, was accosted by a man joyfully exposing himself beside the Water of Leith. He said, 'Come and look at this.'

'At what?' said Jenny, moving closer, thinking to herself he had picked up a fallen nestling from the ground or had discovered a strange plant. Having perceived the truth, she escaped unharmed and unpursued though breathless, and was presently surrounded by solicitous, horrified relations and was coaxed to sip tea well sugared against the shock. Later in the day, since the incident had been reported to the police, came a wonderful policewoman to question Jenny.

These events contained enough exciting possibilities to set the rest of the Easter holidays spinning like a top and to last out the whole of the summer term. The first effect on Sandy was an adverse one, for she had been on the point of obtaining permission to go for walks alone in just such isolated spots as that in which Jenny's encounter had taken place. Sandy was now still forbidden lone walks, but this was a mere by-effect of the affair. The rest brought nothing but good. The subject fell under two headings: first, the man himself and the nature of what he had exposed to view, and secondly the policewoman.

The first was fairly quickly exhausted.

'He was a horrible creature,' said Jenny.

'A terrible beast,' said Sandy.

The question of the policewoman was inexhaustible, and although Sandy never saw her, nor at that time any policewoman (for these were in the early days of the women police), she quite deserted Alan Breck and Mr Rochester and all the heroes of fiction for the summer term, and fell in love with the unseen policewoman who had questioned Jenny; and in this way she managed to keep alive Jenny's enthusiasm too.

'What did she look like? Did she wear a helmet?'

'No, a cap. She had short, fair, curly hair curling under the cap. And a dark blue uniform. She said, "Now tell me all about it."'

'And what did you say?' said Sandy for the fourth time.

For the fourth time Jenny replied: 'Well, I said, "The man was walking along under the trees by the bank, and he was holding something in his hand. And then when he saw me he laughed out loud and said, come and look at this. I said, at what? And I went a bit closer and I saw ..." –

but I couldn't tell the policewoman what I saw, could I?
So the policewoman said to me, "You saw something
nasty?" And I said "yes". Then she asked me what the
man was like, and . . .'

But this was the same story all over again. Sandy wanted
new details about the policewoman, she looked for clues.
Jenny had pronounced the word 'nasty' as 'nesty', which
was unusual for Jenny.

'Did she say "nasty" or "nesty"?' said Sandy on this
fourth telling.

'Nesty.'

This gave rise to an extremely nasty feeling in Sandy
and it put her off the idea of sex for months. All the more as
she disapproved of the pronunciation of the word, it made
her flesh creep, and she plagued Jenny to change her mind
and agree that the policewoman had pronounced it properly.

'A lot of people say nesty,' said Jenny.

'I know, but I don't like them. They're neither one thing
nor another.'

It bothered Sandy a great deal, and she had to invent a
new speaking-image for the policewoman. Another thing
that troubled her was that Jenny did not know the policewoman's name, or even whether she was addressed as 'con-
stable', 'sergeant', or merely 'miss'. Sandy decided to call
her Sergeant Anne Grey. Sandy was Anne Grey's right-
hand woman in the Force, and they were dedicated to
eliminate sex from Edinburgh and environs. In the Sunday
newspapers, to which Sandy had free access, the correct
technical phrases were to be found, such as 'intimacy took
place' and 'plaintiff was in a certain condition'. Females
who were up for sex were not called 'Miss' or 'Mrs', they
were referred to by their surnames: 'Willis was remanded
in custody . . .' 'Roebuck', said Counsel, 'was discovered to
be in a certain condition.'

So Sandy pushed her dark blue police force cap to the

back of her head and sitting on a stile beside Sergeant Anne Grey watched the spot between the trees by the Water of Leith where the terrible beast had appeared who had said 'Look at this' to Jenny, but where, in fact, Sandy never was.

'And another thing,' said Sandy, 'we've got to find out more about the case of Brodie and whether she is yet in a certain condition as a consequence of her liaison with Gordon Lowther, described as singing master, Marcia Blaine School for Girls.'

'Intimacy has undoubtedly taken place,' said Sergeant Anne, looking very nice in her dark uniform and short-cropped curls blondely fringing her cap. She said, 'All we need are a few incriminating documents.'

'Leave all that to me, Sergeant Anne,' said Sandy, because she was at that very time engaged with Jenny in composing the love correspondence between Miss Brodie and the singing master. Sergeant Anne pressed Sandy's hand in gratitude; and they looked into each other's eyes, their mutual understanding too deep for words.

At school after the holidays the Water of Leith affair was kept a secret between Jenny and Sandy, for Jenny's mother had said the story must not be spread about. But it seemed natural that Miss Brodie should be told in a spirit of sensational confiding.

But something made Sandy say to Jenny on the first afternoon of the term: 'Don't tell Miss Brodie.'

'Why?' said Jenny.

Sandy tried to work out the reason. It was connected with the undecided state of Miss Brodie's relationship to cheerful Mr Lowther, and with the fact that she had told her class, first thing: 'I have spent Easter at the little Roman village of Cramond.' That was where Mr Lowther lived all alone in a big house with a housekeeper.

'Don't tell Miss Brodie,' said Sandy.

'Why?' said Jenny.

Sandy made a further effort to work out her reasons. They were also connected with something that had happened in the course of the morning, when Miss Brodie, wanting a supply of drawing books and charcoal to start the new term, sent Monica Douglas to fetch them from the art room, then called her back, and sent Rose Stanley instead. When Rose returned, laden with drawing books and boxes of chalks, she was followed by Teddy Lloyd, similarly laden. He dumped his books and asked Miss Brodie if she had enjoyed her holiday. She gave him her hand, and said she had been exploring Cramond, one should not neglect these little nearby seaports.

'I shouldn't have thought there was much to *explore* at Cramond,' said Mr Lloyd, smiling at her with his golden forelock falling into his eye.

'It has quite a lot of charm,' she said. 'And did you go away at all?'

'I've been painting,' he said in his hoarse voice. 'Family portraits.'

Rose had been stacking the drawing books into their cupboard and now she had finished. As she turned, Miss Brodie put her arm round Rose's shoulder and thanked Mr Lloyd for his help, as if she and Rose were one.

'N'tall,' said Mr Lloyd, meaning 'Not at all', and went away. It was then Jenny whispered, 'Rose has changed in the holidays, hasn't she?'

This was true. Her fair hair was cut shorter and was very shiny. Her cheeks were paler and thinner, her eyes less wide open, set with the lids half-shut as if she were posing for a special photograph.

'Perhaps she has got the Change,' said Sandy. Miss Brodie called it the Menarche but so far when they tried to use this word amongst themselves it made them giggle and feel shy.

Later in the afternoon after school, Jenny said: 'I'd better tell Miss Brodie about the man I met.'

Sandy replied, 'Don't tell Miss Brodie.'

'Why not?' said Jenny.

Sandy tried, but could not think why not, except to feel an unfinished quality about Miss Brodie and her holiday at Cramond, and her sending Rose to Mr Lloyd. So she said, 'The policewoman said to try to forget what happened. Perhaps Miss Brodie would make you remember it.'

Jenny said, 'That's what I think, too.'

And so they forgot the man by the Water of Leith and remembered the policewoman more and more as the term wore on.

During the last few months of Miss Brodie's teaching she made herself adorable. She did not exhort or bicker and even when hard pressed was irritable only with Mary Macgregor. That spring she monopolized with her class the benches under the elm from which could be seen an endless avenue of dark pink May trees, and heard the trotting of horses in time to the turning wheels of light carts returning home empty by a hidden lane from their early morning rounds. Not far off, like a promise of next year, a group of girls from the Senior school were doing first-form Latin. Once, the Latin mistress was moved by the spring of the year to sing a folk-song to fit the clip-clop of the ponies and carts, and Miss Brodie held up her index finger with delight so that her own girls should listen too.

> Nundinarum adest dies,
> Mulus ille nos vehet.
> Eie, curre, mule, mule,
> I tolutari gradu.

That spring Jenny's mother was expecting a baby, there was no rain worth remembering, the grass, the sun and the birds lost their self-centred winter mood and began to think of others. Miss Brodie's old love story was newly embroidered, under the elm, with curious threads: it appeared that while on leave from the war, her late fiancé had frequently taken her out sailing in a fishing boat and that they had spent some of their merriest times among the rocks and pebbles of a small seaport. 'Sometimes Hugh would sing, he had a rich tenor voice. At other times he fell silent and would set up his easel and paint. He was very talented at both arts, but I think the painter was the real Hugh.'

This was the first time the girls had heard of Hugh's artistic leanings. Sandy puzzled over this and took counsel with Jenny, and it came to them both that Miss Brodie was making her new love story fit the old. Thereafter the two girls listened with double ears, and the rest of the class with single.

Sandy was fascinated by this method of making patterns with facts, and was divided between her admiration for the technique and the pressing need to prove Miss Brodie guilty of misconduct.

'What about those incriminating documents?' said Sergeant Anne Grey in her jolly friendly manner. She really was very thrilling.

Sandy and Jenny completed the love correspondence between Miss Brodie and the singing master at half-term. They were staying in the small town of Crail on the coast of Fife with Jenny's aunt who showed herself suspicious of their notebook: and so they took it off to a neighbouring village along the coast by bus, and sat at the mouth of a cave to finish the work. It had been a delicate question how to present Miss Brodie in both a favourable and an unfavourable light, for now, as their last term with Miss Brodie drew to a close, nothing less than this was demanded.

That intimacy had taken place was to be established. But not on an ordinary bed. That had been a thought suitable only for the enlivening of a sewing period, but Miss Brodie was entitled to something like a status. They placed Miss Brodie on the lofty lion's back of Arthur's Seat, with only the sky for roof and bracken for a bed. The broad parkland rolled away beneath her gaze to the accompanying flash and crash of a thunderstorm. It was here that Gordon Lowther, shy and smiling, small with a long body and short legs, his red-gold hair and moustache, found her.

'Took her,' Jenny had said when they had first talked it over.

'Took her – well, no. She gave herself to him.'

'She gave herself to him,' Jenny said, 'although she would fain have given herself to another.'

The last letter in the series, completed at mid-term, went as follows:

My Own Delightful Gordon,

Your letter has moved me deeply as you may imagine. But alas, I must ever decline to be Mrs Lowther. My reasons are twofold. I am dedicated to my Girls as is Madame Pavlova, and there is another in my life whose mutual love reaches out to me beyond the bounds of Time and Space. He is Teddy Lloyd! Intimacy has never taken place with him. He is married to another. One day in the art room we melted into each other's arms and knew the truth. But I was proud of giving myself to you when you came and took me in the bracken on Arthur's Seat while the storm raged about us. If I am in a certain condition I shall place the infant in the care of a worthy shepherd and his wife, and we can discuss it calmly as platonic acquaintances. I may permit misconduct to occur again from time to time as an outlet because I am in my Prime. We can also have many a breezy day in the fishing boat at sea.

I wish to inform you that your housekeeper fills me with anxiety like John Knox. I fear she is rather narrow, which arises from an ignorance of culture and the Italian scene. Pray ask her not to say 'You know your way up' when I call at your house at Cramond. She should take me up and show me in. Her knees are not stiff. She is only pretending that they are.

I love to hear you singing 'Hey Johnnie Cope'. But were I to receive a proposal of marriage tomorrow from the Lord Lyon King-of-Arms I would decline it.

Allow me, in conclusion, to congratulate you warmly upon your sexual intercourse, as well as your singing.

With fondest joy,
Jean Brodie

When they had finished writing this letter they read the whole correspondence from beginning to end. They were undecided then whether to cast this incriminating document out to sea or to bury it. The act of casting things out to sea from the shore was, as they knew, more difficult than it sounded. But Sandy found a damp hole half-hidden by a stone at the back of the cave and they pressed into it the notebook containing the love correspondence of Miss Jean Brodie, and never saw it again. They walked back to Crail over the very springy turf full of fresh plans and fondest joy.

Chapter Four

'I have enough gunpowder in this jar to blow up this school,' said Miss Lockhart in even tones.

She stood behind her bench in her white linen coat, with both hands on a glass jar three-quarters full of a dark grey powder. The extreme hush that fell was only what she expected, for she always opened the first science lesson with these words and with the gunpowder before her, and the first science lesson was no lesson at all, but a naming of the most impressive objects in the science room. Every eye was upon the jar. Miss Lockhart lifted it and placed it carefully in a cupboard which was filled with similar jars full of different coloured crystals and powders.

'These are bunsen burners, this is a test-tube, this is a pipette, that's a burette, that is a retort, a crucible . . .'

Thus she established her mysterious priesthood. She was quite the nicest teacher in the Senior School. But they were all the nicest teachers in the school. It was a new life altogether, almost a new school. Here were no gaunt mistresses like Miss Gaunt, those many who had stalked past Miss Brodie in the corridors saying 'good morning' with predestination in their smiles. The teachers here seemed to have no thoughts of anyone's personalities apart from their speciality in life, whether it was mathematics, Latin or science. They treated the new first-formers as if they were not real, but only to be dealt with, like symbols of algebra, and Miss Brodie's pupils found this refreshing at first. Wonderful, too, during the first week was the curriculum of dazzling new subjects, and the rushing to and from room to room to keep to the time-table. Their days were now filled with unfamiliar shapes and sounds which were magically dissociated from ordinary life, the great circles and triangles of geometry, the hieroglyphics of Greek on the page and the curious hisses and spits some of the Greek sounds made from the teacher's lips – 'psst . . . psooch . . .'

A few weeks later, when meanings appeared from among these sighs and sounds, it was difficult to remember the party-game effect of that first week, and that Greek had ever made hisses and spits or that 'mensarum' had sounded like something out of nonsense verse. The Modern side, up to the third form, was distinguished from the Classical only by modern or ancient languages. The girls on the Modern side were doing German and Spanish, which, when rehearsed between periods, made the astonishing noises of foreign stations got in passing on the wireless. A mademoiselle with black frizzy hair, who wore a striped shirt with real cufflinks, was pronouncing French in a foreign way which never really caught on. The science room smelt unevenly of the Canongate on that day of the winter's walk with Miss Brodie, the bunsen burners, and the sweet autumnal smoke that drifted in from the first burning leaves Here in the science room – strictly not to be referred to as a laboratory – lessons were called experiments, which gave everyone the feeling that not even Miss Lockhart knew what the result might be, and anything might occur between their going in and coming out and the school might blow up.

Here, during that first week, an experiment was conducted which involved magnesium in a test-tube which was made to tickle a bunsen flame. Eventually, from different parts of the room, great white magnesium flares shot out of the test-tubes and were caught in larger glass vessels which waited for the purpose Mary Macgregor took fright and ran along a single lane between two benches, met with a white flame, and ran back to meet another brilliant tongue of fire. Hither and thither she ran in panic between the benches until she was caught and induced to calm down, and she was told not to be so stupid by Miss Lockhart, who already had learnt the exasperation of looking at Mary's face, its two eyes, nose and mouth, with nothing more to say about it.

Once, in later years, when Sandy was visited by Rose Stanley, and they fell to speaking of dead Mary Macgregor, Sandy said,

'When any ill befalls me I wish I had been nicer to Mary.'

'How were we to know?' said Rose.

And Miss Brodie, sitting in the window of the Braid Hills Hotel with Sandy, had said: 'I wonder if it was Mary Macgregor betrayed me? Perhaps I should have been kinder to Mary.'

The Brodie set might easily have lost its identity at this time, not only because Miss Brodie had ceased to preside over their days which were now so brisk with the getting of knowledge from unsoulful experts, but also because the headmistress intended them to be dispersed.

She laid a scheme and it failed. It was too ambitious, it aimed at ridding the school of Miss Brodie and breaking up the Brodie set in the one stroke.

She befriended Mary Macgregor, thinking her to be gullible and bribable, and underrating her stupidity. She remembered that Mary had, in common with all Miss Brodie's girls, applied to go on the Classical side, but had been refused. Now Miss Mackay changed her mind and allowed her to take at least Latin. In return she expected to be informed concerning Miss Brodie. But as the only reason that Mary had wanted to learn Latin was to please Miss Brodie, the headmistress got no further. Give the girl tea as she might, Mary simply did not understand what was required of her and thought all the teachers were in league together, Miss Brodie and all.

'You won't be seeing much of Miss Brodie,' said Miss Mackay, 'now that you are in the Senior school.'

'I see,' said Mary, taking the remark as an edict rather than a probing question.

Miss Mackay laid another scheme and the scheme undid her. There was a highly competitive house system in the Senior school, whose four houses were named Holyrood, Melrose, Argyll and Biggar. Miss Mackay saw to it that the Brodie girls were as far as possible placed in different houses. Jenny was put in Holyrood, Sandy with Mary Macgregor in Melrose, Monica and Eunice went into Argyll and Rose Stanley into Biggar. They were therefore obliged to compete with each other in every walk of life within the school and on the wind-swept hockey fields which lay like the graves of the martyrs exposed to the weather in an outer suburb. It was the team spirit, they were told, that counted now, every house must go all out for the Shield and turn up on Saturday mornings to yell encouragement to the house. Inter-house friendships must not suffer, of course, but the team spirit . . .

This phrase was enough for the Brodie set who, after two years at Miss Brodie's, had been well directed as to its meaning.

'Phrases like "the team spirit" are always employed to cut across individualism, love and personal loyalties,' she had said. 'Ideas like "the team spirit" ', she said, 'ought not to be enjoined on the female sex, especially if they are of that dedicated nature whose virtues from time immemorial have been utterly opposed to the concept. Florence Nightingale knew nothing of the team spirit, her mission was to save life regardless of the team to which it belonged. Cleopatra knew nothing of the team spirit if you read your Shakespeare. Take Helen of Troy. And the Queen of England, it is true she attends international sport, but she has to, it is all empty show, she is concerned only with the King's health and antiques. Where would the team spirit have got Sybil Thorndike? *She* is the great actress and the rest of the cast have got the team spirit. Pavlova . . .'

Perhaps Miss Brodie had foreseen this moment of the future when her team of six should be exposed to the appeal of four different competing spirits, Argyll, Melrose, Biggar and Holyrood. It was impossible to know how much Miss Brodie planned by deliberation, or how much she worked by instinct alone. However, in this, the first test of her strength, she had the victory. Not one of the senior house-prefects personified an argument to touch Sybil Thorndike and Cleopatra. The Brodie set would as soon have entered the Girl Guides as the team spirit. Not only they, but at least ten other girls who had passed through Brodie hands kept away from the playing grounds except under compulsion. No one, save Eunice Gardiner, got near to being put in any team to try her spirit upon. Everyone agreed that Eunice was so good on the field, she could not help it.

On most Saturday afternoons Miss Brodie entertained her old set to tea and listened to their new experiences. Herself, she told them, she did not think much of her new pupils' potentialities, and she described some of her new little girls and made the old ones laugh, which bound her set together more than ever and made them feel chosen. Sooner or later she inquired what they were doing in the art class, for now the girls were taught by golden-locked, one-armed Teddy Lloyd.

There was always a great deal to tell about the art lesson. Their first day, Mr Lloyd found difficulty in keeping order. After so many unfamiliar packed hours and periods of different exact subjects, the girls immediately felt the relaxing nature of the art room, and brimmed over with relaxation. Mr Lloyd shouted at them in his hoarse voice to shut up. This was most bracing.

He was attempting to explain the nature and appearance of an ellipse by holding up a saucer in his one right hand, high above his head, then lower. But his romantic air and his hoarse 'Shut up' had produced a reaction of giggles varying in tone and pitch.

'If you girls don't shut up I'll smash this saucer to the floor,' he said.

They tried but failed to shut up.

He smashed the saucer to the floor.

Amid the dead silence which followed he picked on Rose Stanley and indicating the fragments of saucer on the floor, he said, 'You with the profile – pick this up.'

He turned away and went and did something else at the other end of the long room for the rest of the period, while the girls looked anew at Rose Stanley's profile, marvelled at Mr Lloyd's style, and settled down to drawing a bottle set up in front of a curtain. Jenny remarked to Sandy that Miss Brodie really had good taste.

'He has an artistic temperament, of course,' said Miss Brodie when she was told about the saucer. And when she heard that he had called Rose 'you with the profile', she looked at Rose in a special way, while Sandy looked at Miss Brodie.

The interest of Sandy and Jenny in Miss Brodie's lovers had entered a new phase since they had buried their last composition and moved up to the Senior school. They no longer saw everything in a sexual context, it was now rather a question of plumbing the deep heart's core. The world of pure sex seemed years away. Jenny had turned twelve. Her mother had recently given birth to a baby boy, and the event had not moved them even to speculate upon its origin.

'There's not much time for sex research in the Senior school,' Sandy said.

'I feel I'm past it,' said Jenny. This was strangely true, and she did not again experience her early sense of erotic wonder in life until suddenly one day when she was nearly forty, an actress of moderate reputation married to a theatrical manager. It happened she was standing with a man whom she did not know very well outside a famous building in Rome, waiting for the rain to stop. She was surprised by a reawakening of that same buoyant and airy discovery of sex, a total sensation which it was impossible to say was physical or mental, only that it contained the lost and guileless delight of her eleventh year. She supposed herself to have fallen in love with the man, who might, she thought, have been moved towards her in his own way out of a world of his own, the associations of which were largely unknown to her. There was nothing whatever to be done about it, for Jenny had been contentedly married for sixteen years past; but the concise happening filled her with astonishment whenever it came to mind in later days, and with a sense of the hidden possibilities in all things.

'Mr Lowther's housekeeper,' said Miss Brodie one Saturday afternoon, 'has left him. It is most ungrateful, that house at Cramond is easily run. I never cared for her as you know. I think she resented my position as Mr Lowther's friend and confidante, and seemed dissatisfied by my visits. Mr Lowther is composing some music for song at the moment. He ought to be encouraged.'

The next Saturday she told the girls that the sewing sisters, Miss Ellen and Miss Alison Kerr, had taken on the temporary task of housekeepers to Mr Lowther, since they lived near Cramond.

'I think those sisters are inquisitive,' Miss Brodie remarked. 'They are too much in with Miss Gaunt and the Church of Scotland.'

On Saturday afternoons an hour was spent on her Greek lessons, for she had insisted that Jenny and Sandy should teach her Greek at the same time as they learned it. 'There is an old tradition for this practice,' said Miss Brodie. 'Many families in the olden days could afford to send but one child to school, whereupon that one scholar of the family imparted to the others in the evening what he had learned in the morning. I have long wanted to know the Greek language, and this scheme will also serve to impress your knowledge on your own minds. John Stuart Mill used to rise at dawn to learn Greek at the age of five, and what John Stuart Mill could do as an infant at dawn, I too can do on a Saturday afternoon in my prime.'

She progressed in Greek, although she was somewhat muddled about the accents, being differently informed by Jenny and Sandy who took turns to impart to her their weekly intake of the language. But she was determined to enter and share the new life of her special girls, and what she did not regard as humane of their new concerns, or what was not within the scope of her influence, she scorned.

She said: 'It is witty to say that a straight line is the shortest distance between two points, or that a circle is a plane figure bounded by one line, every point of which is equidistant from a fixed centre. It is plain witty. Everyone knows what a straight line and a circle are.'

When, after the examinations at the end of the first term, she looked at the papers they had been set, she read some of the more vulnerable of the questions aloud with the greatest contempt: 'A window cleaner carries a uniform 60-lb. ladder 15 ft long, at one end of which a bucket of water weighing 40 lb. is hung. At what point must he support the ladder to carry it horizontally? Where is the c.g. of his load?' Miss Brodie looked at the paper, after reading out this question as if to indicate that she could not believe her eyes. Many a time she gave the girls to understand that the solution to such problems would be quite useless to Sybil Thorndike, Anna Pavlova and the late Helen of Troy.

But the Brodie set were on the whole still dazzled by their new subjects. It was never the same in later years when the languages of physics and chemistry, algebra and geometry had lost their elemental strangeness and formed each an individual department of life with its own accustomed boredom, and become hard work. Even Monica Douglas, who later developed such a good brain for mathematics, was plainly never so thrilled with herself as when she first subtracted x from y and the result from a; she never afterwards looked so happy.

Rose Stanley sliced a worm down the middle with the greatest absorption during her first term's biology, although in two terms' time she shuddered at the thought and had dropped the subject. Eunice Gardiner discovered the Industrial Revolution, its rights and wrongs, to such an extent that the history teacher, a vegetarian communist, had high hopes of her which were dashed within a few months when Eunice reverted to reading novels based on the life of Mary Queen of Scots. Sandy, whose handwriting was bad, spent hours forming the Greek characters in neat rows in her notebooks while Jenny took the same pride in drawing scientific apparatus for her chemistry notes. Even stupid Mary Macgregor amazed herself by understanding Caesar's Gallic Wars which as yet made no demands on her defective imagination and the words of which were easier to her than English to spell and pronounce, until suddenly one day it appeared, from an essay she had been obliged to write, that she believed the document to date from the time of Samuel Pepys; and then Mary was established in the wrong again, being tortured with probing questions, and generally led on to confess to the mirth-shaken world her notion that Latin and shorthand were one.

Miss Brodie had a hard fight of it during those first few months when the Senior school had captivated her set, displaying as did the set that capacity for enthusiasm which she herself had implanted. But, having won the battle over the team spirit, she did not despair. It was evident even then that her main concern was lest the girls should become personally attached to any one of the senior teachers, but she carefully refrained from direct attack because the teachers themselves seemed so perfectly indifferent to her brood.

By the summer term, the girls' favourite hours were those spent unbrainfully in the gymnasium, swinging about on parallel bars, hanging upside down on wall bars or climbing ropes up to the ceiling, all competing with agile Eunice to heave themselves up by hands, knees, and feet like monkeys climbing a tropical creeper, while the gym teacher, a thin grey-haired little wire, showed them what to do and shouted each order in a broad Scots accent interspersed by her short cough, on account of which she was later sent to a sanatorium in Switzerland.

By the summer term, to stave off the onslaughts of boredom, and to reconcile the necessities of the working day with their love for Miss Brodie, Sandy and Jenny had begun to apply their new-found knowledge to Miss Brodie in a merry fashion. 'If Miss Brodie was weighed in air and then in water ...' And, when Mr Lowther seemed not quite himself at the singing lesson, they would remind each other that an immersed Jean Brodie displaces its own weight of Gordon Lowther.

Presently, in the late spring of nineteen-thirty-three, Miss Brodie's Greek lessons on a Saturday afternoon came to an end, because of the needs of Mr Lowther who, in his house at Cramond which the girls had not yet seen, was being catered for quite willingly by those sewing mistresses, Miss Ellen and Miss Alison Kerr. Living on the coast nearby, it was simple for them to go over turn by turn and see to Mr Lowther after school hours, and prepare his supper and lay out provision for his breakfast; it was not only simple, it was enjoyable to be doing good, and it was also profitable in a genteel way. On Saturdays either Miss Ellen or Miss Alison would count his laundry and keep house for him. On some Saturday mornings both were busy for him; Miss Ellen supervised the woman who came to clean while Miss Alison did the week's shopping. They never had been so perky or useful in their lives before, and especially not since the eldest sister had died, who had always told them what to do with their spare time as it cropped up, so that Miss Alison could never get used to being called Miss Kerr and Miss Ellen could never find it in her to go and get a book from the library, wanting the order from the late Miss Kerr.

But the minister's sister, gaunt Miss Gaunt, was secretly taking over the dead sister's office. As it became known later, Miss Gaunt approved of their arrangement with Gordon

Lowther and encouraged them to make it a permanent one for their own good and also for private reasons connected with Miss Brodie.

Up to now, Miss Brodie's visits to Mr. Lowther had taken place on Sundays. She always went to church on Sunday mornings, she had a rota of different denominations and sects which included the Free Churches of Scotland, the Established Church of Scotland, the Methodist and the Episcopalian churches and any other church outside the Roman Catholic pale which she might discover. Her disapproval of the Church of Rome was based on her assertions that it was a church of superstition, and that only people who did not want to think for themselves were Roman Catholics. In some ways, her attitude was a strange one, because she was by temperament suited only to the Roman Catholic Church; possibly it could have embraced, even while it disciplined, her soaring and diving spirit, it might even have normalized her. But perhaps this was the reason that she shunned it, lover of Italy though she was, bringing to her support a rigid Edinburgh-born side of herself when the Catholic Church was in question, although this side was not otherwise greatly in evidence. So she went round the various non-Roman churches instead, hardly ever missing a Sunday morning. She was not in any doubt, she let everyone know she was in no doubt, that God was on her side whatever her course, and so she experienced no difficulty or sense of hypocrisy in worship while at the same time she went to bed with the singing master. Just as an excessive sense of guilt can drive people to excessive action, so was Miss Brodie driven to it by an excessive lack of guilt.

The side-effects of this condition were exhilarating to her special girls in that they in some way partook of the general absolution she had assumed to herself, and it was only in retrospect that they could see Miss Brodie's affair with Mr Lowther for what it was, that is to say, in a factual light. All the time they were under her influence she and her actions were outside the context of right and wrong. It was twenty-five years before Sandy had so far recovered from a creeping vision of disorder that she could look back and recognize that Miss Brodie's defective sense of self-criticism had not been without its beneficent and enlarging effects; by which time Sandy had already betrayed Miss Brodie and Miss Brodie was laid in her grave.

It was after morning church on Sundays that Miss Brodie would go to Cramond, there to lunch and spend the afternoon with Mr Lowther. She spent Sunday evenings with him also, and more often than not the night, in a spirit of definite duty, if not exactly martyrdom, since her heart was with the renounced teacher of art.

Mr Lowther, with his long body and short legs, was a shy fellow who smiled upon nearly everyone from beneath his red-gold moustache, and who won his own gentle way with nearly everybody, and who said little and sang much.

When it became certain that the Kerr sisters had taken over permanently the housekeeping for this bashful, smiling bachelor, Miss Brodie fancied he was getting thin. She announced this discovery just at a time when Jenny and Sandy had noticed a slimmer appearance in Miss Brodie and had begun to wonder, since they were nearly thirteen and their eyes were more focused on such points, if she might be physically beautiful or desirable to men. They saw her in a new way, and decided she had a certain deep romantic beauty, and that she had lost weight through her sad passion for Mr Lloyd, and this noble undertaking of Mr Lowther in his place, and that it suited her.

Now Miss Brodie was saying: 'Mr Lowther is looking thin these days. I have no faith in those Kerr sisters, they are skimping him, they have got skimpy minds. The supplies of food they leave behind on Saturdays are barely sufficient to see him through Sunday, let alone the remainder of the week. If only Mr Lowther could be persuaded to move from that big house and take a flat in Edinburgh, he would be so much easier to look after. He needs looking after. But he will not be persuaded. It is impossible to persuade a man who does not disagree, but smiles.'

She decided to supervise the Kerr sisters on their Saturdays at Cramond when they prepared for Mr Lowther's domestic week ahead. 'They get well paid for it,' said Miss Brodie. 'I shall go over and see that they order the right stuff, and sufficient.' It might have seemed an audacious proposition, but the girls did not think of it this way. They heartily urged Miss Brodie to descend upon the Kerrs and to interfere, partly in anticipation of some eventful consequence, and partly because Mr Lowther would somehow smile away any fuss; and the Kerr sisters were fairly craven; and, above all, Miss Brodie was easily the equal of both sisters together, she was the square on the hypotenuse of a right-angled triangle and they were only the squares on the other two sides.

The Kerr sisters took Miss Brodie's intrusion quite meekly, and that they were so unquestioning about any authority which imposed itself upon them was the very reason why they also did not hesitate later on to answer the subsequent questions of Miss Gaunt. Meantime Miss Brodie set about feeding Mr Lowther up, and, since this meant her passing Saturday afternoons at Cramond, the Brodie set was invited to go, two by two, one pair every week, to visit her in Mr Lowther's residence, where he smiled and patted their hair or pulled pretty Jenny's ringlets, looking meanwhile for reproof or approval, or some such thing, at brown-eyed Jean Brodie. She gave them tea while he smiled; and he frequently laid down his cup and saucer, went and sat at the piano and burst into song. He sang:

> 'March, march, Ettrick and Teviotdale,
> *Why* the de'il dinna ye march *forward* in order?
> March, march, Eskdale and Liddesdale,
> All the Blue Bonnets are bound for the Border.'

At the end of the song he would smile his overcome and bashful smile and take his teacup again, looking up under his ginger eyebrows at Jean Brodie to see what she felt about him at the current moment. She was Jean to him, a fact that none of the Brodie set thought proper to mention to anyone.

She reported to Sandy and Jenny: 'I made short work of those Kerr sisters. They were starving him. Now it is I who see to the provisions. I am a descendant, do not forget, of Willie Brodie, a man of substance, a cabinet maker and designer of gibbets, a member of the Town Council of Edinburgh and a keeper of two mistresses who bore him five children between them. Blood tells. He played much dice and fighting cocks. Eventually he was a wanted man for having robbed the Excise Office – not that he needed the money, he was a night burglar only for the sake of the danger in it. Of course, he was arrested abroad and was brought back to the Tolbooth prison, but that was mere chance. He died cheerfully on a gibbet of his own devising in seventeen-eighty-eight. However all this may be, it is the stuff I am made of, and I have brooked and shall brook no nonsense from Miss Ellen and Miss Alison Kerr.'

Mr Lowther sang:

> 'O mother, mother, make my bed,
> O make it soft and narrow,
> For my true love died for me today.
> I'll die for him tomorrow.'

Then he looked at Miss Brodie. She was, however, looking at a chipped rim of a teacup. 'Mary Macgregor must have chipped it,' she said. 'Mary was here last Sunday with Eunice and they washed up together. Mary must have chipped it.'

Outside on the summer lawn the daisies sparkled. The lawn spread wide and long, one could barely see the little wood at the end of it and even the wood belonged to Mr

Lowther, and the fields beyond. Shy, musical and gentle as he was, Mr Lowther was a man of substance.

Now Sandy considered Miss Brodie not only to see if she was desirable, but also to find out if there was any element of surrender about her, since this was the most difficult part of the affair to realize. She had been a dominant presence rather than a physical woman like Norma Shearer or Elizabeth Bergner. Miss Brodie was now forty-three and this year when she looked so much thinner than when she had stood in the classroom or sat under the elm, her shape was pleasanter, but it was still fairly large compared with Mr Lowther's. He was slight and he was shorter than Miss Brodie. He looked at her with love and she looked at him severely and possessively.

By the end of the summer term, when the Brodie set were all turned, or nearly turned, thirteen, Miss Brodie questioned them in their visiting pairs each week about their art lesson. The girls always took a close interest in Teddy Lloyd's art classes and in all he did, making much of details, so as to provide happy conversation with Miss Brodie when their turn came to visit her at Gordon Lowther's house at Cramond.

It was a large gabled house with a folly-turret. There were so many twists and turns in the wooded path leading up from the road, and the front lawn was so narrow, that the house could never be seen from the little distance that its size demanded and it was necessary to crane one's neck upward to see the turret at all. The back of the house was quite plain. The rooms were large and gloomy with Venetian blinds. The banisters began with a pair of carved lions' heads and carried up and up, round and round, as far as the eye could reach. All the furniture was large and carved, dotted with ornaments of silver and rose-coloured glass. The library on the ground floor where Miss Brodie entertained them held a number of glass bookcases so dim in their interiors that it was impossible to see the titles of the books without peering close. A grand piano was placed across one corner of the room, and on it, in summer, stood a bowl of roses.

This was a great house to explore and on days when Miss Brodie was curiously occupied in the kitchen with some enormous preparation for the next day's eating – in those months when her obsession with Mr Lowther's food had just begun – the girls were free to roam up the big stairs, hand-in-hand with awe, and to open the doors and look into the dust-sheeted bedrooms and especially into two rooms that people had forgotten to furnish properly, one of which had nothing in it but a large desk, not even a carpet, the other of which was empty except for an electric light bulb and a large blue jug. These rooms were icy cold, whatever the time of year. On their descending the stairs after these expeditions, Mr Lowther would often be standing waiting for them, shyly smiling in the hall with his hands clasped together as if he hoped that everything was to their satisfaction. He took roses from the bowl and presented one each to the girls before they went home.

Mr Lowther never seemed quite at home in his home, although he had been born there. He always looked at Miss Brodie for approval before he touched anything or opened a cupboard as if, really, he was not allowed to touch without permission. The girls decided that perhaps his mother, now four years dead, had kept him under all his life, and he was consequently unable to see himself as master of the house.

He sat silently and gratefully watching Miss Brodie entertain the two girls whose turn it was to be there, when she had already started on her project of fattening him up which was to grow to such huge proportions that her food-supplying mania was the talk of Miss Ellen and Miss Alison Kerr, and so of the Junior school. One day, when Sandy and Jenny were on the visiting rota, she gave Mr Lowther, for tea alone, an admirable lobster salad, some sandwiches of liver paste, cake and tea, followed by a bowl of porridge and cream. These were served to him on a tray for himself alone, you could see he was on a special diet. Sandy was anxious to see if Mr Lowther would manage the porridge as well as everything else. But he worked his way through everything with impassive obedience while she questioned the girls: 'What are you doing in the art class just now?'

'We're at work on the poster competition.'

'Mr Lloyd – is he well?'

'Oh yes, he's great fun. He showed us his studio two weeks ago.'

'Which studio, where? At his house?' – although Miss Brodie knew perfectly well.

'Yes, it's a great long attic, it –'

'Did you meet his wife, what was she like? What did she say, did she give you tea? What are the children like, what did you do when you got there? . . .'

She did not attempt to conceal from her munching host her keen interest in the art master. Mr Lowther's eyes looked mournful as he ate on. Sandy and Jenny knew that similar questions had been pressed upon Mary Macgregor and Eunice Gardiner the previous week, and upon Rose Stanley and Monica Douglas the week before. But Miss Brodie could not hear enough versions of the same story if it involved Teddy Lloyd, and now that the girls had been to his house – a large and shabby, a warm and unconventional establishment in the north of Edinburgh – Miss Brodie was in a state of high excitement by very contact with these girls who had lately breathed Lloyd air.

'How many children?' said Miss Brodie, her teapot poised.

'Five, I think,' said Sandy.

'Six, I think,' said Jenny, 'counting the baby.'

'There are lots of babies.' said Sandy.

'Roman Catholics, of course,' said Miss Brodie, addressing this to Mr Lowther.

'But the littlest baby,' said Jenny, 'you've forgotten to count the wee baby. That makes six.'

Miss Brodie poured tea and cast a glance at Gordon Lowther's plate.

'Gordon,' she said, 'a cake.'

He shook his head and said softly, as if soothing her, 'Oh, no, no.'

'Yes, Gordon. It is full of goodness.' And she made him eat a Chester cake, and spoke to him in a slightly more Edinburgh way than usual, so as to make up to him by both means for the love she was giving to Teddy Lloyd instead of to him.

'You must be fattened up, Gordon,' she said. 'You must be two stone the better before I go my holidays.'

He smiled as best he could at everyone in turn, with his drooped head and slowly moving jaws. Meanwhile Miss Brodie said:

'And Mrs Lloyd – is she a woman, would you say, in her prime?'

'Perhaps not yet,' said Sandy.

'Well, Mrs Lloyd may be past it,' Jenny said. 'It's difficult to say with her hair being long on her shoulders. It makes her look young although she may not be.'

'She looks really like as if she won't have any prime,' Sandy said.

'The word "like" is redundant in that sentence. What is Mrs Lloyd's Christian name?'

'Deirdre,' said Jenny, and Miss Brodie considered the name as if it were new to her although she had heard it last week from Mary and Eunice, and the week before that from Rose and Monica and so had Mr Lowther. Outside, light rain began to fall on Mr Lowther's leaves.

'Celtic,' said Miss Brodie.

Sandy loitered at the kitchen door waiting for Miss

Brodie to come for a walk by the sea. Miss Brodie was doing something to an enormous ham prior to putting it into a huge pot. Miss Brodie's new ventures into cookery in no way diminished her previous grandeur, for everything she prepared for Gordon Lowther seemed to be large, whether it was family-sized puddings to last him out the week, or joints of beef or lamb, or great angry-eyed whole salmon.

'I must get this on for Mr Lowther's supper,' she said to Sandy, 'and see that he gets his supper before I go home tonight.'

She always so far kept up the idea that she went home on these week-end nights and left Mr Lowther alone in the big house. So far the girls had found no evidence to the contrary, nor were they ever to do so; a little later Miss Ellen Kerr was brought to the headmistress by Miss Gaunt to testify to having found Miss Brodie's nightdress under a pillow of the double bed on which Mr Lowther took his sleep. She had found it while changing the linen; it was the pillow on the far side of the bed, nearest the wall, under which the nightdress had been discovered folded neatly.

'How do you know the nightdress was Miss Brodie's?' demanded Miss Mackay, the sharp-minded woman, who smelt her prey very near and yet saw it very far. She stood with a hand on the back of her chair, bending forward full of ears.

'One must draw one's own conclusions,' said Miss Gaunt.

'I am addressing Miss Ellen.'

'Yes, one must draw one's own conclusions,' said Miss Ellen, with her tight-drawn red-veined cheeks looking shiny and flustered. 'It was crêpe de Chine.'

'It is non-proven,' said Miss Mackay, sitting down to her desk. 'Come back to me,' she said, 'if you have proof positive. What did you do with the garment? Did you confront Miss Brodie with it?'

'Oh, no, Miss Mackay,' said Miss Ellen.

'You should have confronted her with it. You should have said, "Miss Brodie, come here a minute, can you explain this?" That's what you should have said. Is the nightdress still there?'

'Oh, no, it's gone.'

'She's that brazen,' said Miss Gaunt.

All this was conveyed to Sandy by the headmistress herself at that subsequent time when Sandy looked at her distastefully through her little eyes and, evading the quite crude question which the coarse-faced woman asked her, was moved by various other considerations to betray Miss Brodie.

'But I must organize the dear fellow's food before I go home tonight,' Miss Brodie said in the summer of nineteen-thirty-three while Sandy leaned against the kitchen door with her legs longing to be running along the sea shore. Jenny came and joined her, and together they waited upon Miss Brodie, and saw on the vast old kitchen table the piled-up provisions of the morning's shopping. Outside on the dining-room table stood large bowls of fruit with boxes of dates piled on top of them, as if this were Christmas and the kitchen that of a holiday hotel.

'Won't all this give Mr Lowther a stoppage?' Sandy said to Jenny.

'Not if he eats his greens,' said Jenny.

While they waited for Miss Brodie to dress the great ham like the heroine she was, there came the sound of Mr Lowther at the piano in the library singing rather slowly and mournfully:

> 'All people that on earth do dwell,
>   Sing to the Lord with cheerful voice.
> Him serve with mirth, his praise forth tell,
>   Come ye before him and rejoice.'

Mr Lowther was the choir-master and an Elder of the church, and had not yet been quietly advised to withdraw

94

from these offices by Mr Gaunt the minister, brother of Miss Gaunt, following the finding of the nightdress under the pillow next to his.

Presently, as she put the ham on a low gas and settled the lid on the pot Miss Brodie joined in the psalm richly, contralto-wise, giving the notes more body:

> 'O enter then his gates with praise,
> Approach with joy His courts unto.'

The rain had stopped and was only now hanging damply within the salt air. All along the sea front Miss Brodie questioned the girls, against the rhythm of the waves, about the appointments of Teddy Lloyd's house, the kind of tea they got, how vast and light was the studio, and what was said.

'He looked very romantic in his own studio,' Sandy said.

'How was that?'

'I think it was his having only one arm,' said Jenny.

'But he always has only one arm.'

'He did more than usual with it,' said Sandy.

'He was waving it about,' Jenny said. 'There was a lovely view from the studio window. He's proud of it.'

'The studio is in the attic, I presume?'

'Yes, all along the top of the house. There is a new portrait he has done of his family, it's a little bit amusing, it starts with himself, very tall, then his wife. Then all the little children graded downwards to the baby on the floor, it makes a diagonal line across the canvas.'

'What makes it amusing?' said Miss Brodie.

'They are all facing square and they all look serious,' Sandy said. 'You are supposed to laugh at it.'

Miss Brodie laughed a little at this. There was a wonderful sunset across the distant sky, reflected in the sea, streaked with blood and puffed with avenging purple and gold as if the end of the world had come without intruding on every-day life.

'There's another portrait,' Jenny said, 'not finished yet, of Rose.'

'He has been painting Rose?'

'Yes.'

'Rose has been sitting for him?'

'Yes, for about a month.'

Miss Brodie was very excited. 'Rose didn't mention this,' she said.

Sandy halted. 'Oh, I forgot. It was supposed to be a surprise. You aren't supposed to know.'

'What, the portrait, I am to see it?'

Sandy looked confused, for she was not sure how Rose had meant her portrait to be a surprise to Miss Brodie.

Jenny said, 'Oh, Miss Brodie, it is the fact that she's sitting for Mr Lloyd that she wanted to keep for a surprise.' Sandy realized, then, that this was right.

'Ah' said Miss Brodie, well pleased. 'That is thoughtful of Rose.'

Sandy was jealous, because Rose was not supposed to be thoughtful.

'What is she wearing for her portrait?' said Miss Brodie.

'Her gym tunic,' Sandy said.

'Sitting sideways,' Jenny said.

'In profile,' said Miss Brodie.

Miss Brodie stopped a man to buy a lobster for Mr Lowther. When this was done she said:

'Rose is bound to be painted many times. She may well sit for Mr Lloyd on future occasions, she is one of the crème de la crème.'

It was said in an inquiring tone. The girls understood she was trying quite hard to piece together a whole picture from their random remarks.

Jenny accordingly let fall, 'Oh, yes, Mr Lloyd wants to paint Rose in red velvet.'

And Sandy added, 'Mrs Lloyd has a bit of red velvet to put around her, they were trying it round her.'

'Are you to return?' said Miss Brodie.

'Yes, all of us,' Sandy said. 'Mr Lloyd thinks we're a jolly nice set.'

'Have you not thought it remarkable,' said Miss Brodie, 'that it is you six girls that Mr Lloyd has chosen to invite to his studio?'

'Well, we're a set,' said Jenny.

'Has he invited any other girls from the school?' – but Miss Brodie knew the answer.

'Oh, no, only us.'

'It is because you are mine,' said Miss Brodie. 'I mean of my stamp and cut, and I am in my prime.'

Sandy and Jenny had not given much thought to the fact of the art master's inviting them as a group. Indeed, there was something special in his acceptance of the Brodie set. There was a mystery here to be worked out, and it was clear that when he thought of them he thought of Miss Brodie.

'He always asks about you,' Sandy said to Miss Brodie, 'as soon as he sees us.'

'Yes, Rose did tell me that,' said Miss Brodie.

Suddenly, like migrating birds, Sandy and Jenny were of one mind for a run and without warning they ran along the pebbly beach into the air which was full of sunset, returning to Miss Brodie to hear of her forthcoming summer holiday when she was going to leave the fattened-up Mr Lowther, she was afraid, to fend for himself with the aid of the Misses Kerr, and was going abroad, not to Italy this year but to Germany, where Hitler was become Chancellor, a prophet-figure like Thomas Carlyle, and more reliable than Mussolini; the German brownshirts, she said, were exactly the same as the Italian black, only more reliable.

Jenny and Sandy were going to a farm for the summer holidays, where in fact the name of Miss Brodie would not very much be on their lips or in their minds after the first two weeks, and instead they would make hay and follow the sheep about. It was always difficult to realize during term times that the world of Miss Brodie might be half forgotten, as were the worlds of the school houses, Holyrood, Melrose, Argyll and Biggar.

'I wonder if Mr Lowther would care for sweetbreads done with rice,' Miss Brodie said.

Chapter Five

'Why, it's like Miss Brodie!' said Sandy. 'It's terribly like Miss Brodie.' Then, perceiving that what she had said had accumulated a meaning between its passing her lips and reaching the ears of Mr and Mrs Lloyd, she said, 'Though of course it's Rose, it's more like Rose, it's terribly like Rose.'

Teddy Lloyd shifted the new portrait so that it stood in a different light. It still looked like Miss Brodie.

Deirdre Lloyd said, 'I haven't met Miss Brodie, I think. Is she fair?'

'No,' said Teddy Lloyd in his hoarse way, 'she's dark.'

Sandy saw that the head on the portrait was fair, it was Rose's portrait all right. Rose was seated in profile by a window in her gym dress, her hands palm-downwards, one on each knee. Where was the resemblance to Miss Brodie? It was the profile perhaps; it was the forehead, perhaps; it was the type of stare from Rose's blue eyes, perhaps, which was like the dominating stare from Miss Brodie's brown. The portrait was very like Miss Brodie.

'It's Rose, all right,' Sandy said, and Deirdre Lloyd looked at her.

'Do you like it?' said Teddy Lloyd.

'Yes, it's lovely.'

'Well, that's all that matters.'

Sandy continued looking at it through her very small eyes, and while she was doing so Teddy Lloyd drew the piece of sheeting over the portrait with a casual flip of his only arm.

Deirdre Lloyd had been the first woman to dress up as a peasant whom Sandy had ever met, and peasant women were to be fashionable for the next thirty years or more. She wore a fairly long full-gathered dark skirt, a bright green blouse with the sleeves rolled up, a necklace of large painted wooden beads, and gipsy-looking ear-rings. Round her waist was a bright red wide belt. She wore dark brown stockings and sandals of dark green suede. In this, and various other costumes of similar kind, Deirdre was depicted on canvas in different parts of the studio. She had an attractive near-laughing voice. She said:

'We've got a new one of Rose. Teddy, show Sandy the new one of Rose.'

'It isn't quite at a stage for looking at.'

'Well, what about Red Velvet? Show Sandy that – Teddy did a splendid portrait of Rose last summer, we swathed her in red velvet, and we've called it Red Velvet.'

Teddy Lloyd had brought out a canvas from behind a few others. He stood it in the light on an easel. Sandy looked at it with her tiny eyes which it was astonishing that anyone could trust.

The portrait was like Miss Brodie. Sandy said, 'I like the colours.'

'Does it resemble Miss Brodie?' said Deirdre Lloyd with her near-laughter.

'Miss Brodie is a woman in her prime,' said Sandy, 'but there is a resemblance now you mention it.'

Deirdre Lloyd said: 'Rose was only fourteen at the time; it makes her look very mature, but indeed she is very mature.'

The swathing of crimson velvet was so arranged that it did two things at once, it made Rose look one-armed like the artist himself, and it showed the curves of her breast to be more developed than they were, even now, when Rose was fifteen. Also, the picture was like Miss Brodie, and this was the main thing about it and the main mystery. Rose had a large-boned pale face. Miss Brodie's bones were small, although her eyes, nose and mouth were large. It was difficult to see how Teddy Lloyd had imposed the dark and Roman face of Miss Brodie on that of pale Rose, but he had done so.

Sandy looked again at the other recent portraits in the studio, Teddy Lloyd's wife, his children, some unknown sitters. They were none of them like Miss Brodie.

Then she saw a drawing lying on top of a pile on the work-table. It was Miss Brodie leaning against a lamp post in the Lawnmarket with a working-woman's shawl around her; on looking closer it proved to be Monica Douglas with the high cheekbones and long nose. Sandy said:

'I didn't know Monica sat for you.'

'I've done one or two preliminary sketches. Don't you think that setting's rather good for Monica? Here's one of Eunice in her harlequin outfit, I thought she looked rather well in it.'

Sandy was vexed. These girls, Monica and Eunice, had not said anything to the others about their being painted by the art master. But now they were all fifteen there was a lot they did not tell each other. She looked more closely at this picture of Eunice.

Eunice had worn the harlequin dress for a school performance. Small and neat and sharp-featured as she was, in the portrait she looked like Miss Brodie. In amongst her various bewilderments Sandy was fascinated by the economy of Teddy Lloyd's method, as she had been four years earlier by Miss Brodie's variations on her love story, when she had attached to her first, war-time lover the attributes of the art master and the singing master who had then newly entered her orbit. Teddy Lloyd's method of presentation was similar, it was economical, and it always seemed afterwards to Sandy that where there was a choice of various courses, the most economical was the best, and that the course to be taken was the most expedient and most suitable at the time for all the objects in hand. She acted on this principle when the time came for her to betray Miss Brodie.

Jenny had done badly in her last term's examinations and was mostly, these days, at home working up her subjects. Sandy had the definite feeling that the Brodie set, not to mention Miss Brodie herself, was getting out of hand. She thought it perhaps a good thing that the set might split up.

From somewhere below one of the Lloyd children started to yell, and then another, and then a chorus. Deirdre Lloyd disappeared with a swing of her peasant skirt to see to all her children. The Lloyds were Catholics and so were made to have a lot of children by force.

'One day,' said Teddy Lloyd as he stacked up his sketches before taking Sandy down to tea, 'I would like to do all you Brodie girls, one by one and then all together.' He tossed his head to move back the golden lock of his hair from his eye. 'It would be nice to do you all together,' he said, 'and see what sort of a group portrait I could make of you.'

Sandy thought this might be an attempt to keep the Brodie set together at the expense of the newly glimpsed individuality of its members. She turned on him in her new manner of sudden irritability and said, 'We'd look like one big Miss Brodie, I suppose.'

He laughed in a delighted way and looked at her more closely, as if for the first time. She looked back just as closely through her little eyes, with the near-blackmailing insolence of her knowledge. Whereupon he kissed her long and wetly. He said in his hoarse voice, 'That'll teach you to look at an artist like that.'

She started to run to the door, wiping her mouth dry with the back of her hand, but he caught her with his one arm and said: 'There's no need to run away. You're just about the ugliest little thing I've ever seen in my life.' He walked out and left her standing in the studio, and there was nothing for her to do but to follow him downstairs. Deirdre Lloyd's voice called from the sitting-room. 'In here, Sandy.'

She spent most of the tea time trying to sort out her preliminary feelings in the matter, which was difficult because of the children who were present and making demands on the guest. The eldest boy, who was eight, turned on the wireless and began to sing in mincing English tones, 'Oh play to me, Gipsy' to the accompaniment of Henry Hall's band. The other three children were making various kinds of din. Above this noise Deirdre Lloyd requested Sandy to call her Deirdre rather than Mrs Lloyd. And so Sandy did not have much opportunity to discover how she was feeling inside herself about Teddy Lloyd's kiss and his words, and to decide whether she was insulted or not. He now said, brazenly, 'And you can call me Teddy outside of school.' Amongst themselves, in any case, the girls called him Teddy the Paint. Sandy looked from one to the other of the Lloyds.

'I've heard such a lot about Miss Brodie from the girls,' Deirdre was saying. 'I really must ask her to tea. D'you think she'd like to come?'

'No,' said Teddy.

'Why?' said Deirdre, not that it seemed to matter, she was so languid and long-armed, lifting the plate of biscuits from the table and passing them round without moving from the low stool on which she sat.

'You kids stop that row or you leave the room,' Teddy declared.

'Bring Miss Brodie to tea,' Deirdre said to Sandy.

'She won't come,' Teddy said, ' – will she, Sandy?'

'She's awfully busy,' Sandy said.

'Pass me a fag,' said Deirdre.

'Is she still looking after Lowther?' said Teddy.

'Well, yes, a bit —'

'Lowther,' said Teddy, waving his only arm, 'must have

103

a way with women. He's got half the female staff of the school looking after him. Why doesn't he employ a housekeeper? He's got plenty of money, no wife, no kids, no rent to pay, it's his own house. Why doesn't he get a proper housekeeper?'

'I think he likes Miss Brodie,' Sandy said.

'But what does she see in him?'

'He sings to her,' Sandy said, suddenly sharp.

Deirdre laughed. 'Miss Brodie sounds a bit queer, I must say. What age is she?'

'Jean Brodie,' said Teddy, 'is a magnificent woman in her prime.' He got up, tossing back his lock of hair, and left the room.

Deirdre blew a cloud of reflective smoke and stubbed out her cigarette, and Sandy said she would have to go now.

Mr Lowther had caused Miss Brodie a good deal of worry in the past two years. There had been a time when it seemed he might be thinking of marrying Miss Alison Kerr, and another time when he seemed to favour Miss Ellen, all the while being in love with Miss Brodie herself, who refused him all but her bed-fellowship and her catering.

He tired of food, for it was making him fat and weary and putting him out of voice. He wanted a wife to play golf with and to sing to. He wanted a honeymoon on the Hebridean island of Eigg, near Rum, and then to return to Cramond with the bride.

In the midst of this dissatisfaction had occurred Ellen Kerr's finding of a nightdress of quality folded under the pillow next to Mr Lowther's in that double bed on which, to make matters worse, he had been born.

Still Miss Brodie refused him. He fell into a melancholy mood upon his retirement from the offices of choir-master and Elder, and the girls thought he brooded often upon the possibility that Miss Brodie could not take to his short legs, and was all the time pining for Teddy Lloyd's long ones.

Most of this Miss Brodie obliquely confided in the girls as they grew from thirteen to fourteen and from fourteen to fifteen. She did not say, even obliquely, that she slept with the singing master, for she was still testing them out to see whom she could trust, as it would be her way to put it. She did not want any alarming suspicions to arise in the minds of their parents. Miss Brodie was always very careful to impress the parents of her set and to win their approval and gratitude. So she confided according to what seemed expedient at the time, and was in fact now on the look-out for a girl amongst her set in whom she could confide entirely, whose curiosity was greater than her desire to make a sensation outside, and who, in the need to gain further confidences from Miss Brodie, would never betray what had been gained. Of necessity there had to be but one girl; two would be dangerous. Almost shrewdly, Miss Brodie fixed on Sandy, and even then it was not of her own affairs that she spoke.

In the summer of nineteen-thirty-five the whole school was forced to wear rosettes of red, white and blue ribbons in the lapels of its blazers, because of the Silver Jubilee. Rose Stanley lost hers and said it was probably in Teddy Lloyd's studio. This was not long after Sandy's visit to the art master's residence.

'What are you doing for the summer holidays, Rose?' said Miss Brodie.

'My father's taking me to the Highlands for a fortnight. After that, I don't know. I suppose I'll be sitting for Mr Lloyd off and on.'

'Good,' said Miss Brodie.

Miss Brodie started to confide in Sandy after the next summer holidays. They played rounds of golf in the sunny early autumn after school.

'All my ambitions,' said Miss Brodie, 'are fixed on yourself and Rose. You will not speak of this to the other girls, it would cause envy. I had hopes of Jenny, she is so pretty; but Jenny has become insipid, don't you think?'

This was a clever question, because it articulated what was already growing in Sandy's mind. Jenny had bored her this last year, and it left her lonely.

'Don't you think?' said Miss Brodie, towering above her, for Sandy was playing out of a bunker. Sandy gave a hack with her niblick and said, 'Yes, a bit,' sending the ball in a little backward half-circle.

'And I had hopes of Eunice,' Miss Brodie said presently, 'but she seems to be interested in some boy she goes swimming with.'

Sandy was not yet out of the bunker. It was sometimes difficult to follow Miss Brodie's drift when she was in her prophetic moods. One had to wait and see what emerged. In the meantime she glanced up at Miss Brodie who was standing on the crest of the bunker which was itself on a crest of the hilly course. Miss Brodie looked admirable in her heather-blue tweed with the brown of a recent holiday in Egypt still warming her skin. Miss Brodie was gazing out over Edinburgh as she spoke.

Sandy got out of the bunker. 'Eunice,' said Miss Brodie, 'will settle down and marry some professional man. Perhaps I have done her some good. Mary, well Mary. I never had any hopes of Mary. I thought, when you were young children, that Mary might be something. She was a little pathetic. But she's really a most irritating girl, I'd rather deal with a rogue than a fool. Monica will get her B.Sc. with honours I've no doubt, but she has no spiritual insight, and of course that's why she's – '

Miss Brodie was to drive off now and she had decided to stop talking until she had measured her distance and swiped her ball. Which she did. '– that's why she has a bad temper, she understands nothing but signs and symbols and calculations. Nothing infuriates people more than their own lack of spiritual insight, Sandy, that is why the Moslems are so placid, they are full of spiritual insight. My dragoman in Egypt would not have it that Friday was their Lord's Day. "Every day is the Lord's day," he said to me. I thought that very profound, I felt humbled. We had already said our farewells on the day before my departure, Sandy, but lo and behold when I was already seated in the train, along the platform came my dragoman with a beautiful bunch of flowers for me. He had true dignity. Sandy, you will never get anywhere by hunching over your putter, hold your shoulders back and bend from the waist. He was a very splendid person with a great sense of his bearing.'

They picked up their balls and walked to the next tee.

'Have you ever played with Miss Lockhart?' Sandy said.

'Does she play golf?'

'Yes, rather well.' Sandy had met the science mistress surprisingly on the golf course one Saturday morning playing with Gordon Lowther.

'Good shot, Sandy. I know very little of Miss Lockhart,' said Miss Brodie. 'I leave her to her jars and gases. They are all gross materialists, these women in the Senior school, they all belong to the Fabian Society and are pacifists. That's the sort of thing Mr Lowther, Mr Lloyd and myself are up against when we are not up against the narrow-minded, half-educated crowd in the junior departments. Sandy, I'll swear you are short-sighted, the way you peer at people. You must get spectacles.'

'I'm not,' said Sandy irritably, 'it only seems so.'

'It's unnerving,' said Miss Brodie. 'Do you know, Sandy dear, all my ambitions are for you and Rose. You have got insight, perhaps not quite spiritual, but you're a deep one, and Rose has got instinct, Rose has got instinct.'

'Perhaps not quite spiritual,' said Sandy.

'Yes,' said Miss Brodie, 'you're right. Rose has got a future by virtue of her instinct.'

'She has an instinct how to sit for her portrait,' said Sandy.

'That's what I mean by your insight,' said Miss Brodie. 'I ought to know, because my prime has brought me instinct and insight, both.'

Fully to savour her position, Sandy would go and stand outside St Giles Cathedral or the Tolbooth, and contemplate these emblems of a dark and terrible salvation which made the fires of the damned seem very merry to the imagination by contrast, and much preferable. Nobody in her life, at home or at school, had ever spoken of Calvinism except as a joke that had once been taken seriously. She did not at the time understand that her environment had not been on the surface peculiar to the place, as was the environment of the Edinburgh social classes just above or, even more, just below her own. She had no experience of social class at all. In its outward forms her fifteen years might have been spent in any suburb of any city in the British Isles; her school, with its alien house system, might have been in Ealing. All she was conscious of now was that some quality of life peculiar to Edinburgh and nowhere else had been going on unbeknown to her all the time, and however undesirable it might be, she felt deprived of it; however undesirable, she desired to know what it was, and to cease to be protected from it by enlightened people.

In fact, it was the religion of Calvin of which Sandy felt deprived, or rather a specified recognition of it. She desired this birthright; something definite to reject. It pervaded the place in proportion as it was unacknowledged. In some ways the most real and rooted people whom Sandy knew were Miss Gaunt and the Kerr sisters who made no evasions about their belief that God had planned for practically everybody before they were born a nasty surprise when they died. Later, when Sandy read John Calvin, she found that although popular conceptions of

Calvinism were sometimes mistaken, in this particular there was no mistake, indeed it was but a mild understanding of the case, he having made it God's pleasure to implant in certain people an erroneous sense of joy and salvation, so that their surprise at the end might be the nastier.

Sandy was unable to formulate these exciting propositions; nevertheless she experienced them in the air she breathed, she sensed them in the curiously defiant way in which the people she knew broke the Sabbath, and she smelt them in the excesses of Miss Brodie in her prime. Now that she was allowed to go about alone, she walked round the certainly forbidden quarters of Edinburgh to look at the blackened monuments and hear the unbelievable curses of drunken men and women, and comparing their faces with the faces from Morningside and Merchiston with which she was familiar, she saw, with stabs of new and exciting Calvinistic guilt, that there was not much difference.

In this oblique way, she began to sense what went to the makings of Miss Brodie who had elected herself to grace in so particular a way and with more exotic suicidal enchantment than if she had simply taken to drink like other spinsters who couldn't stand it any more.

It was plain that Miss Brodie wanted Rose with her instinct to start preparing to be Teddy Lloyd's lover, and Sandy with her insight to act as informant on the affair. It was to this end that Rose and Sandy had been chosen as the crème de la crème. There was a whiff of sulphur about the idea which fascinated Sandy in her present mind. After all, it was only an idea. And there was no pressing hurry in the matter, for Miss Brodie liked to take her leisure over the unfolding of her plans, most of her joy deriving from the preparation, and moreover, even if these plans were as clear to her own mind as they were to Sandy's, the girls were too young. All the same, by the time the girls were sixteen Miss Brodie was saying to her set at large: 'Sandy will make an excellent Secret Service agent, a great spy';

and to Sandy alone she had started saying 'Rose will be a great lover. She is above the common moral code, it does not apply to her. This is a fact which it is not expedient for anyone to hear about who is not endowed with insight.'

For over a year Sandy entered into the spirit of this plan, for she visited the Lloyds' frequently, and was able to report to Miss Brodie how things were going with the portraits of Rose which so resembled Miss Brodie.

'Rose,' said Miss Brodie, 'is like a heroine from a novel by D. H. Lawrence. She has got instinct.'

But in fact the art master's interest in Rose was simply a professional one, she was a good model; Rose had an instinct to be satisfied with this role, and in the event it was Sandy who slept with Teddy Lloyd and Rose who carried back the information.

It was some time before these things came to pass, and meanwhile Miss Brodie was neglecting Mr Lowther at Cramond and spending as much time as possible with Rose and Sandy discussing art, and then the question of sitting for an artist, and Rose's future as a model, and the necessity for Rose to realize the power she had within her, it was a gift and she an exception to all the rules, she was the exception that proved the rule. Miss Brodie was too cautious to be more precise and Rose only half-guessed at Miss Brodie's meaning, for she was at this time, as Sandy knew, following her instinct and becoming famous for sex among the schoolboys who stood awkwardly with their bicycles at a safe distance from the school gates. Rose was greatly popular with these boys, which was the only reason why she was famed for sex, although she did not really talk about sex, far less indulge it. She did everything by instinct, she even listened to Miss Brodie as if she agreed with every word.

'When you are seventeen or eighteen, Rose, you will come to the moment of your great fulfilment.'

'Yes, honestly I think so, Miss Brodie.'

Teddy Lloyd's passion for Jean Brodie was greatly in evidence in all the portraits he did of the various members of the Brodie set. He did them in a group during one summer term, wearing their panama hats each in a different way, each hat adorning, in a magical transfiguration, a different Jean Brodie under the forms of Rose, Sandy, Jenny, Mary, Monica and Eunice. But mostly it was Rose, because she was instinctively a good model and Teddy Lloyd paid her five shillings a sitting, which Rose found useful, being addicted to the cinema.

Sandy felt warmly towards Miss Brodie at those times when she saw how she was misled in her idea of Rose. It was then that Miss Brodie looked beautiful and fragile, just as dark heavy Edinburgh itself could suddenly be changed into a floating city when the light was a special pearly white and fell upon one of the gracefully fashioned streets. In the same way Miss Brodie's masterful features became clear and sweet to Sandy when viewed in the curious light of the woman's folly, and she never felt more affection for her in her later years than when she thought upon Miss Brodie as silly.

But Miss Brodie as the leader of the set, Miss Brodie as a Roman matron, Miss Brodie as an educational reformer were still prominent. It was not always comfortable, from the school point of view, to be associated with her. The lack of team spirit alone, the fact that the Brodie set preferred golf to hockey or netball if they preferred anything at all, were enough to set them apart, even if they had not dented in the crowns of their hats and tilted them backwards or forwards. It was impossible for them to escape from the Brodie set because they were the Brodie set in the eyes of the school. Nominally, they were members of Holyrood, Melrose, Argyll and Biggar, but it had been well known that the Brodie set had no team spirit and did not care which house won the shield. They were not allowed to care.

Their disregard had now become an institution, to be respected like the house system itself. For their own part, and without this reputation, the six girls would have gone each her own way by the time she was in the fourth form and had reached the age of sixteen.

But it was irrevocable, and they made the most of it, and saw that their position was really quite enviable. Everyone thought the Brodie set had more fun than anyone else, what with visits to Cramond, to Teddy Lloyd's studio, to the theatre and teas with Miss Brodie. And indeed it was so. And Miss Brodie was always a figure of glamorous activity even in the eyes of the non-Brodie girls.

Miss Brodie's struggles with the authorities on account of her educational system were increasing throughout the years, and she made it a moral duty for her set to rally round her each time her battle reached a crisis. Then she would find them, perhaps, loitering with the bicycle boys after school, and the bicycles would rapidly bear the boys away, and they would be bidden to supper the following evening.

They went to the tram-car stop with her. 'It has been suggested again that I should apply for a post at one of the progressive, that is to say, crank schools. I shall not apply for a post at a crank school. I shall remain at this education factory where my duty lies. There needs must be a leaven in the lump. Give me a girl at an impressionable age and she is mine for life. The gang who oppose me shall not succeed.'

'No,' said everyone. 'No, of course they won't.'

The headmistress had not quite given up testing the girls of the Brodie set to see what they knew. In her frustration she sometimes took reprisals against them when she could do so under the guise of fair play, which was not often.

'If they do not try to unseat me on the grounds of my educational policy, they attempt personal calumny,' said

Miss Brodie one day. 'It is unfortunate, but true, that there have been implications against my character in regard to my relations with poor Mr Lowther. As you girls well know, I have given much of my energy to Mr Lowther's health. I am fond of Mr Lowther. Why not? Are we not bidden to love one another? I am Gordon Lowther's closest friend, his confidante. I have neglected him of late I am afraid, but still I have been all things to Gordon Lowther, and I need only lift my little finger and he would be at my side. This relationship has been distorted . . . .'

It was some months, now, that Miss Brodie had neglected the singing master, and the girls no longer spent Saturday afternoons at Cramond. Sandy assumed that the reason why Miss Brodie had stopped sleeping with Gordon Lowther was that her sexual feelings were satisfied by proxy; and Rose was predestined to be the lover of Teddy Lloyd. 'I have had much calumny to put up with on account of my good offices at Cramond,' said Miss Brodie. 'However, I shall survive it. If I wished I could marry him tomorrow.'

The morning after this saying, the engagement of Gordon Lowther to Miss Lockhart, the science teacher, was announced in *The Scotsman*. Nobody had expected it. Miss Brodie was greatly taken aback and suffered untimely, for a space, from a sense of having been betrayed. But she seemed to recall herself to the fact that the true love of her life was Teddy Lloyd whom she had renounced; and Gordon Lowther had merely been useful. She subscribed with the rest of the school to the china tea-set which was presented to the couple at the last assembly of the term. Mr Lowther made a speech in which he called them 'you girlies', glancing shyly from time to time at Miss Brodie who was watching the clouds through the window. Sometimes he looked towards his bride to be, who stood quietly by the side of the headmistress half-way up the hall waiting till he should be finished and they could join him on the platform. He had confidence in Miss Lockhart, as everyone did, she not only played golf well and drove a car, she could also blow up the school with her jar of gunpowder and would never dream of doing so.

Miss Brodie's brown eyes were fixed on the clouds, she looked quite beautiful and frail, and it occurred to Sandy that she had possibly renounced Teddy Lloyd only because she was aware that she could not keep up this beauty; it was a quality in her that came and went.

Next term, when Mr Lowther returned from his honeymoon on the island of Eigg, Miss Brodie put her spare energy into her plan for Sandy and Rose, with their insight and instinct; and what energy she had to spare from that she now put into political ideas.

Chapter Six

Miss Mackay, the headmistress, never gave up pumping the Brodie set. She knew it was useless to do so directly, her approach was indirect, in the hope that they would be tricked into letting fall some piece of evidence which could be used to enforce Miss Brodie's retirement. Once a term, the girls went to tea with Miss Mackay.

But in any case there was now very little they could say without implicating themselves. By the time their friendship with Miss Brodie was of seven years' standing, it had worked itself into their bones, so that they could not break away without, as it were, splitting their bones to do so.

'You still keep up with Miss Brodie?' said Miss Mackay, with a gleaming smile. She had new teeth.

'Oh, yes, rather . . .'

'Yes, oh yes, from time to time . . .'

Miss Mackay said to Sandy confidentially when her turn came round – because she treated the older girls as equals, which is to say, as equals definitely wearing school uniform – 'Dear Miss Brodie, she sits on under the elm, telling her remarkable life story to the junior children. I mind when Miss Brodie first came to the school, she was a vigorous young teacher, but now –' She sighed and shook her head. She had a habit of putting the universal wise saws into Scots dialect to make them wiser. Now she said, 'What canna be cured maun be endured. But I fear Miss Brodie is past her best. I doubt her class will get through its qualifying examination this year. But don't think I'm criticizing Miss Brodie. She likes her wee drink, I'm sure. After all, it's nobody's business, so long as it doesn't affect her work and you girls.'

'She doesn't drink,' said Sandy, 'except for sherry on her birthday, half a bottle between the seven of us.'

Miss Mackay could be observed mentally scoring drink off her list of things against Miss Brodie. 'Oh, that's all I meant,' said Miss Mackay.

The Brodie girls, now that they were seventeen, were able to detach Miss Brodie from her aspect of teacher. When they conferred amongst themselves on the subject they had to admit, at last, and without doubt, that she was really an exciting woman as a woman. Her eyes flashed, her nose arched proudly, her hair was still brown, and coiled matriarchally at the nape of her neck. The singing master, well satisfied as he was with Miss Lockhart, now Mrs Lowther and lost to the school, would glance at Miss Brodie from under his ginger eyebrows with shy admiration and memories whenever he saw her.

One of her greatest admirers was the new girl called Joyce Emily Hammond who had been sent to Blaine School as a last hope, having been obliged to withdraw from a range of expensive schools north and south of the border, because of her alleged delinquency which so far had not been revealed, except once or twice when she had thrown paper pellets at Mr Lowther and succeeded only in hurting his feelings. She insisted on calling herself Joyce Emily, was brought to school in the morning by a chauffeur in a large black car, though she was obliged to make her own way home; she lived in a huge house with a stables in the near environs of Edinburgh. Joyce Emily's parents, wealthy as they were, had begged for a trial period to elapse before investing in yet another set of school uniform clothing for their daughter. So Joyce Emily still went about in dark green, while the rest wore deep violet, and she boasted five sets of discarded colours hanging in her wardrobe at home besides such relics of governesses as a substantial switch of hair cut off by Joyce Emily's own hand, a post office savings book belonging to a governess called Miss Michie, and the charred remains of a pillow-case upon which the head of yet another governess called Miss Chambers had been resting when Joyce Emily had set fire to it.

The rest of the girls listened to her chatter, but in general she was disapproved of not only because of her green stockings and skirt, her shiny car and chauffeur, but because life was already exceedingly full of working for examinations and playing for the shield. It was the Brodie set to which Joyce Emily mostly desired to attach herself, perceiving their individualism; but they, less than anybody, wanted her. With the exception of Mary Macgregor, they were, in fact, among the brightest girls in the school, which was somewhat a stumbling-block to Miss Mackay in her efforts to discredit Miss Brodie.

The Brodie set, moreover, had outside interests. Eunice had a boy friend with whom she practised swimming and diving. Monica Douglas and Mary Macgregor went slum-visiting together with bundles of groceries, although Mary was reported to be always making remarks like, 'Why don't they eat cake?' (What she actually said was, 'Well, why don't they send their clothes to the laundry?' when she heard complaints of the prohibitive price of soap.) Jenny was already showing her dramatic talent and was all the time rehearsing for something in the school dramatic society. Rose modelled for Teddy Lloyd and Sandy occasionally joined her, and was watchful, and sometimes toyed with the idea of inducing Teddy Lloyd to kiss her again just to see if it could be done by sheer looking at him insolently with her little eyes. In addition to these activities the Brodie set were meeting Miss Brodie by twos and threes, and sometimes all together after school. It was at this time, in nineteen-thirty-seven, that she was especially cultivating Rose, and questioning Sandy, and being answered as to the progress of the great love affair presently to take place between Rose and the art master.

So that they had no time to do much about a delinquent

whose parents had dumped her on the school by their influence, even if she was apparently a delinquent in name only. Miss Brodie, however, found time to take her up. The Brodie girls slightly resented this but were relieved that they were not obliged to share the girl's company, and that Miss Brodie took her to tea and the theatre on her own.

One of Joyce Emily's boasts was that her brother at Oxford had gone to fight in the Spanish Civil War. This dark, rather mad girl wanted to go too, and to wear a white blouse and black skirt and march with a gun. Nobody had taken this seriously. The Spanish Civil War was something going on outside in the newspapers and only once a month in the school debating society. Everyone, including Joyce Emily, was anti-Franco if they were anything at all.

One day it was realized that Joyce Emily had not been at school for some days, and soon someone else was occupying her desk. No one knew why she had left until, six weeks later, it was reported that she had run away to Spain and had been killed in an accident when the train she was travelling in had been attacked. The school held an abbreviated form of remembrance service for her.

Mary had gone to be a shorthand typist and Jenny had gone to a school of dramatic art. Only four remained of the Brodie set for the last year. It was hardly like being at school at all, there was so much free time, so many lectures and so much library research outside the school building for the sixth-form girls that it was just a matter of walking in and out. They were deferred to and consulted, and had the feeling that they could, if they wished, run the place.

Eunice was to do modern languages, although she changed her mind a year later and became a nurse. Monica was destined for science, Sandy for psychology. Rose had hung on, not for any functional reason, but because her father thought she should get the best out of her education, even if she was only going to the art school later on, or at the worst, become a model for artists or dress designers. Rose's father played a big part in her life, he was a huge widower, as handsome in his masculine way as was Rose in her feminine, proudly professing himself a cobbler; that was to say, he now owned an extensive shoe-making business. Some years ago, on meeting Miss Brodie he had immediately taken a hearty male interest in her, as so many men did, not thinking her to be ridiculous as might have been expected; but she would have none of Mr Stanley, for he was hardly what she would call a man of culture. She thought him rather carnal. The girls, however, had always guiltily liked Rose's father. And Rose, instinctive as she undoubtedly was, followed her instinct so far as to take on his hard-headed and merry carnality, and made a good marriage soon after she left school. She shook off Miss Brodie's influence as a dog shakes pond-water from its coat.

Miss Brodie was not to know that this would be, and meantime Rose was inescapably famous for sex and was much sought after by sixth-form schoolboys and first-year university students. And Miss Brodie said to Sandy: 'From what you tell me I should think that Rose and Teddy Lloyd will soon be lovers.' All at once Sandy realized that this was not all theory and a kind of Brodie game, in the way that so much of life was unreal talk and game-planning, like the prospects of a war and other theories that people were putting about in the air like pigeons, and one said, 'Yes, of course, it's inevitable.' But this was not theory; Miss Brodie meant it. Sandy looked at her, and perceived that the woman was obsessed by the need for Rose to sleep with the man she herself was in love with; there was nothing new in the idea, it was the reality that was new. She thought of Miss Brodie eight years ago sitting under the elm tree telling her first simple love story and wondered to what extent it was Miss Brodie who had developed complications through-out the years, and to what extent it was her own conception of Miss Brodie that had changed.

During the year past Sandy had continued seeing the Lloyds. She went shopping with Deirdre Lloyd and got herself a folkweave shirt like Deirdre's. She listened to their conversation, at the same time calculating their souls by signs and symbols, as was the habit in those days of young persons who had read books of psychology when listening to older persons who had not. Sometimes, on days when Rose was required to pose naked, Sandy sat with the painter and his model in the studio, silently watching the strange mutations of the flesh on the canvas as they represented an anonymous nude figure, and at the same time resembled Rose, and more than this, resembled Miss Brodie. Sandy had become highly interested in the painter's mind, so involved with Miss Brodie as it was, and not accounting her ridiculous.

'From what you tell me I should think that Rose and Teddy Lloyd will soon be lovers.' Sandy realized that Miss Brodie meant it. She had told Miss Brodie how peculiarly all his portraits reflected her. She had said so again and again, for Miss Brodie loved to hear it. She had said that Teddy Lloyd wanted to give up teaching and was preparing an exhibition, and was encouraged in this course by art critics and discouraged by the thought of his large family.

'I am his Muse,' said Miss Brodie. 'But I have re-nounced his love in order to dedicate my prime to the young girls in my care. I am his Muse but Rose shall take my place.'

She thinks she is Providence, thought Sandy, she thinks she is the God of Calvin, she sees the beginning and the end. And Sandy thought, too, the woman is an unconscious Lesbian. And many theories from the books of psychology categorized Miss Brodie, but failed to obliterate her image from the canvases of one-armed Teddy Lloyd.

When she was a nun, sooner or later one and the other of the Brodie set came to visit Sandy, because it was something to do, and she had written her book of psychology, and everyone likes to visit a nun, it provides a spiritual sensation, a catharsis to go home with, especially if the nun clutches the bars of the grille. Rose came, now long since married to a successful business man who varied in his line of business from canned goods to merchant banking. They fell to talking about Miss Brodie.

'She talked a lot about dedication,' said Rose, 'but she didn't mean your sort of dedication. But don't you think she was dedicated to her girls in a way?'

'Oh yes, I think she was,' said Sandy.

'Why did she get the push?' said Rose. 'Was it sex?'

'No, politics.'

'I didn't know she bothered about politics.'

'It was only a side line,' Sandy said, 'but it served as an excuse.'

Monica Douglas came to visit Sandy because there was a crisis in her life. She had married a scientist and in one of her fits of anger had thrown a live coal at his sister. Whereupon the scientist demanded a separation, once and for all.

'I'm not much good at that sort of problem,' said Sandy. But Monica had not thought she would be able to help much, for she knew Sandy of old, and persons known of old can never be of much help. So they fell to talking of Miss Brodie.

'Did she ever get Rose to sleep with Teddy Lloyd?' said Monica.

'No,' said Sandy.

'Was she in love with Teddy Lloyd herself?'

'Yes,' said Sandy, 'and he was in love with her.'

'Then it was a real renunciation in a way,' said Monica.

'Yes, it was,' said Sandy. 'After all, she was a woman in her prime.'

'You used to think her talk about renunciation was a joke,' said Monica.'

'So did you,' said Sandy.

In the summer of nineteen-thirty-eight, after the last of the Brodie set had left Blaine, Miss Brodie went to Germany and Austria, while Sandy read psychology and went to the Lloyds' to sit for her own portrait. Rose came and kept them company occasionally.

When Deirdre Lloyd took the children into the country Teddy had to stay on in Edinburgh because he was giving a summer course at the art school. Sandy continued to sit for her portrait twice a week, and sometimes Rose came and sometimes not.

One day when they were alone, Sandy told Teddy Lloyd that all his portraits, even that of the littlest Lloyd baby, were now turning out to be likenesses of Miss Brodie, and she gave him her insolent blackmailing stare. He kissed her as he had done three years before when she was fifteen, and for the best part of five weeks of the summer they had a love affair in the empty house, only sometimes answering the door to Rose, but at other times letting the bell scream on.

During that time he painted a little, and she said: 'You are still making me look like Jean Brodie.' So he started a new canvas, but it was the same again.

She said: 'Why are you obsessed with that woman? Can't you see she's ridiculous?'

He said, yes, he could see Jean Brodie was ridiculous. He said, would she kindly stop analysing his mind, it was unnatural in a girl of eighteen.

Miss Brodie telephoned for Sandy to come to see her early in September. She had returned from Germany and Austria which were now magnificently organized. After the war Miss Brodie admitted to Sandy, as they sat in the Braid Hills Hotel, 'Hitler *was* rather naughty,' but at this time she was full of her travels and quite sure the new régime would save the world. Sandy was bored, it did not seem necessary that the world should be saved, only that the poor people in the streets and slums of Edinburgh should be relieved. Miss Brodie said there would be no war. Sandy never had thought so, anyway. Miss Brodie came to the point: 'Rose tells me you have become his lover.'

'Yes, does it matter which one of us it is?'

'Whatever possessed you?' said Miss Brodie in a very Scottish way, as if Sandy had given away a pound of marmalade to an English duke.

'He interests me,' said Sandy.

'Interests you, forsooth,' said Miss Brodie. 'A girl with a mind, a girl with insight. He is a Roman Catholic and I don't see how you can have to do with a man who can't think for himself. Rose was suitable. Rose has instinct but no insight.'

Teddy Lloyd continued reproducing Jean Brodie in his paintings. 'You have instinct,' Sandy told him, 'but no insight, or you would see that the woman isn't to be taken seriously.'

'I know she isn't,' he said. 'You are too analytical and irritable for your age.'

The family had returned and their meetings were dangerous and exciting. The more she discovered him to be still in love with Jean Brodie, the more she was curious about the mind that loved the woman. By the end of the year it happened that she had quite lost interest in the man himself, but was deeply absorbed in his mind, from which she extracted, among other things, his religion as a pith from a husk. Her mind was as full of his religion as a night sky is full of things visible and invisible. She left the man and took his religion and became a nun in the course of time.

But that autumn, while she was still probing the mind that invented Miss Brodie on canvas after canvas, Sandy met Miss Brodie several times. She was at first merely resigned to Sandy's liaison with the art master. Presently she was exultant, and presently again inquired for details, which she did not get.

'His portraits still resemble me?' said Miss Brodie.

'Yes, very much,' said Sandy.

'Then all is well,' said Miss Brodie. 'And after all, Sandy,' she said, 'you are destined to be the great lover, although I would not have thought it. Truth is stranger than fiction. I wanted Rose for him, I admit, and sometimes I regretted urging young Joyce Emily to go to Spain to fight for Franco, she would have done admirably for him, a girl of instinct, a –'

'Did she go to fight for Franco?' said Sandy.

'That was the intention. I made her see sense. However, she didn't have the chance to fight at all, poor girl.'

When Sandy returned, as was expected of her, to see Miss Mackay that autumn, the headmistress said to this rather difficult old girl with the abnormally small eyes, 'You'll have been seeing something of Miss Brodie, I hope. You aren't forgetting your old friends, I hope.'

'I've seen her once or twice,' said Sandy.

'I'm afraid she put ideas into your young heads,' said Miss Mackay with a knowing twinkle, which meant that now Sandy had left school it would be all right to talk openly about Miss Brodie's goings-on.

'Yes, lots of ideas,' Sandy said.

'I wish I knew what some of them were,' said Miss Mackay, slumping a little and genuinely worried. 'Because it is still going on, I mean class after class, and now she has formed a new set, and they are so out of key with the rest of the school, Miss Brodie's set. They are precocious. Do you know what I mean?'

'Yes,' said Sandy. 'But you won't be able to pin her down on sex. Have you thought of politics?'

Miss Mackay turned her chair so that it was nearly square with Sandy's. This was business.

'My dear,' she said, 'what do you mean? I didn't know she was attracted by politics.'

'Neither she is,' said Sandy, 'except as a side interest. She's a born Fascist, have you thought of that?'

'I shall question her pupils on those lines and see what emerges, if that is what you advise, Sandy. I had no idea you felt so seriously about the state of world affairs, Sandy, and I'm more than delighted –'

'I'm not really interested in world affairs,' said Sandy, 'only in putting a stop to Miss Brodie.'

It was clear the headmistress thought this rather unpleasant of Sandy. But she did not fail to say to Miss Brodie, when the time came, 'It was one of your own girls who gave me the tip, one of your set, Miss Brodie.'

Sandy was to leave Edinburgh at the end of the year and when she said goodbye to the Lloyds she looked round the studio at the canvases on which she had failed to put a stop to Miss Brodie. She congratulated Teddy Lloyd on the economy of his method. He congratulated her on the economy of hers, and Deirdre looked to see whatever did he mean? Sandy thought, if he knew about my stopping of Miss Brodie, he would think me more economical still. She was more fuming, now, with Christian morals, than John Knox.

Miss Brodie was forced to retire at the end of the summer term of nineteen-thirty-nine, on the grounds that she had been teaching Fascism. Sandy, when she heard of it, thought of the marching troops of black shirts in the pictures on the wall. By now she had entered the Catholic Church, in whose ranks she had found quite a number of Fascists much less agreeable than Miss Brodie.

'Of course,' said Miss Brodie when she wrote to tell Sandy the news of her retirement, 'this political question was only an excuse. They tried to prove personal immorality against me on many occasions and failed. My girls were always reticent on these matters. It was my educational policy they were up against which had reached its perfection in my prime. I was dedicated to my girls, as you know. But they used this political excuse as a weapon. What hurts and amazes me most of all is the fact, if Miss Mackay is to be believed, that it was one of my own set who betrayed me and put the inquiry in motion.

'You will be astonished. I can write to you of this, because you of all my set are exempt from suspicion, you had no *reason* to betray me. I think first of Mary Macgregor. Perhaps Mary has nursed a grievance, in her stupidity of mind, against me – she is such an exasperating young woman. I think of Rose. It may be that Rose resented my coming first with Mr L. Eunice – I cannot think it could be Eunice, but I did frequently have to come down firmly on her commonplace ideas. She wanted to be a Girl Guide, you remember. She was attracted to the Team Spirit – could it be that Eunice bore a grudge? Then there is Jenny. Now you know Jenny, how she went *off* and was never the same after she wanted to be an actress. She became so dull. Do you think she minded my telling her that she would never be a Fay Compton, far less a Sybil Thorndike? Finally, there is Monica. I half incline to suspect Monica. There is very little Soul behind the mathematical brain, and it may be that, in a fit of rage against that Beauty, Truth and Goodness which was beyond her grasp, she turned and betrayed me.

'You, Sandy, as you see, I exempt from suspicion, since you had no reason whatsoever to betray me, indeed you have had the best part of me in my confidences and in the man I love. Think, if you can, who it could have been. I must know which one of you betrayed me . . .'

Sandy replied like an enigmatic Pope: 'If you did not betray us it is impossible that you could have been betrayed by us. The word betrayed does not apply . . .'

She heard again from Miss Brodie at the time of Mary

Macgregor's death, when the girl ran hither and thither in the hotel fire and was trapped by it. 'If this is a judgement on poor Mary for betraying me, I am sure I would not have wished . . .'

'I'm afraid', Jenny wrote, 'Miss Brodie is past her prime. She keeps wanting to know who betrayed her. It isn't at all like the old Miss Brodie; she was always so full of fight.'

Her name and memory, after her death, flitted from mouth to mouth like swallows in summer, and in winter they were gone. It was always in summer time that the Brodie set came to visit Sandy, for the nunnery was deep in the country.

When Jenny came to see Sandy, who now bore the name Sister Helena of the Transfiguration, she told Sandy about her sudden falling in love with a man in Rome and there being nothing to be done about it. 'Miss Brodie would have liked to know about it,' she said, 'sinner as she was.'

'Oh, she was quite an innocent in her way,' said Sandy, clutching the bars of the grille.

Eunice, when she came, told Sandy, 'We were at the Edinburgh Festival last year. I found Miss Brodie's grave, I put some flowers on it. I've told my husband all the stories about her, sitting under the elm and all that; he thinks she was marvellous fun.'

'So she was, really, when you think of it.'

'Yes, she was,' said Eunice, 'when she was in her prime.'

Monica came again. 'Before she died,' she said, 'Miss Brodie thought it was you who betrayed her.'

'It's only possible to betray where loyalty is due,' said Sandy.

'Well, wasn't it due to Miss Brodie?'

'Only up to a point,' said Sandy.

And there was that day when the inquiring young man came to see Sandy because of her strange book of psychology, 'The Transfiguration of the Commonplace', which had brought so many visitors that Sandy clutched the bars of her grille more desperately than ever.

'What were the main influences of your school days, Sister Helena? Were they literary or political or personal? Was it Calvinism?'

Sandy said: 'There was a Miss Jean Brodie in her prime.'